CAP O' RUSHES

and other folk tales

CAP O' RUSHES
and other folk tales

retold by
WINIFRED FINLAY
Illustrated by Victor Ambrus

E. M. HALE & COMPANY
Eau Claire, Wisconsin

First published in Great Britain by
Kaye & Ward Ltd
21 New Street, London EC2M 4NT
1974
First United States edition, 1974
published by
E. M. Hale & Co. Inc.
1201 South Hastings Way,
Eau Claire, Wisconsin 54701, USA

ISBN 0-8382-1096-1

Printed in Great Britain by
Northumberland Press Limited, Gateshead

CONTENTS

Some of these stories first appeared in
Child Education.

FOR JOHN FARQUHARSON
AND CORDELIA JANE

1

CAP O' RUSHES

There once lived a rich gentleman who had three beautiful daughters: the eldest had dark eyes and hair as black as a raven's wing; the second had red hair and eyes as green as glass; while as for the youngest, her eyes were as blue as the speedwell which grows by the wayside, and her hair, which was so long that she could sit on it, was the pale gold of the primrose when it first appears in the woods in the springtime.

Now, one cold winter's day, the gentleman had occasion to go to London on business, and when he returned later that week he brought with him, as presents for his daughters, three costly gowns.

'Go and put on your gowns now,' he said, sitting down by the side of the big, open fire in the hall, and patting the two hounds which came to lie at his feet.

Eagerly the three daughters went up to their chamber to do as their father bade them. When at length they returned to the hall, the eldest daughter was magnificent in a gown of beaten gold which shimmered and glittered in the candle-light; the second daughter was superb in a silver gown which glimmered and sparkled in the dancing light of the fire; while as for the youngest daughter—whom the gentleman loved most of all—she looked more beautiful than either of her sisters in a gown of white satin embroidered with gold and sewn with sapphires as blue as her eyes.

'Do you like the presents I brought you?' the gentleman asked, whereupon his three daughters kissed him, assuring him that never in their lives had they seen such beautiful gowns.

'And do you think I am a good father to you?' the gentleman continued.

'The best father in the world,' said the eldest daughter.

'The kindest and most generous,' said the second.

But the youngest contented herself with nodding her head and smiling happily at her father.

'I am glad to know I am appreciated,' the gentleman said, 'but what I should really like to know is just how much my beautiful daughters love me.'

'How much?' said the eldest, stroking her gown of beaten gold. 'Why – as much as my life.'

The gentleman smiled with satisfaction.

'How much?' repeated the second, caressing her gown of glimmering silver. 'Why – better than all the world.'

The smile on the gentleman's face grew even more satisfied as he turned to his youngest daughter, whom he loved best of all.

'How much?' said the youngest daughter softly. 'Why – as much as fresh meat loves salt.' And sitting down on her stool, she picked up her embroidery.

'Do you call that an answer?' the gentleman cried, springing to his feet and kicking his hounds out of the way. 'Is that the only answer you can give your father after all the money he has spent on you?'

But the youngest daughter had said her say, and had nothing to add to it.

'Very well!' shouted the gentleman, striding to the door and flinging it open so that the wind rushed in and shook the tapestries on the walls. 'If that's all you think of me, you are no longer my daughter. Go and find yourself a new home and never let me see your face again.'

Without a word the youngest daughter put down her embroidery, rose from her stool by the fire, and walked out into the wind and rain, while behind her, the gentleman closed the door with a thud and shot home the bolts at the top and the bottom.

Whatever shall I do now, the youngest daughter wondered, looking around her in the darkness.

Just at that moment the little scullery maid hurried round

from the back of the house, a lantern in one hand and a cloak in the other.

'You were so kind to me when I first came here and was homesick,' the little maid said. 'Now it is my turn to help you.

'Take this lantern to light you on your way, and take this cloak which my mother wove for me before I left home.

'If you have nowhere to go, then follow the old road which goes east by north until it reaches land that is as flat as a table, where there are only fens and marshes and drifting white mists. Keep on walking until you come to a stone bridge which spans a lazy, grey-green river. At the far side you will see a mansion with towers and turrets, three times as big as your father's house. Go to the back door, and ask the housekeeper if she has any work for you.'

Thanking the little maid warmly, the youngest daughter put on the cloak and, lantern in hand, set off in the darkness along the old road which went east by north. All night she walked, and when the sun rose she found herself in country which was as flat as a table; ditches filled with water cut though the desolate marshes and fens, and all that grew there were a few stunted trees, green moss, white bog cotton, and long rushes with flat, green spears. At last she came to a stone bridge which spanned a lazy, grey-green river and, through the drifting mists, she saw on the far side a mansion with towers and turrets, three times as big as her father's house.

I can't ask the housekeeper for work if I look like this, the youngest daughter thought. Hurrying down to the river bank, she gathered an armful of the longest and greenest and strongest rushes, and these she wove into a cloak and hood. Taking off the cloak which the little maid had given her and the silken gown which her father had brought her from London, she smeared dirt over her hands and face and hair, and then she put on the cloak and hood which she had fashioned for herself from the rushes, wrapped her

silken gown in the little maid's cloak to keep it clean, and
set off for the mansion with towers and turrets.

When she knocked at the back door, the only person
stirring at the time was a scullion, a mean, bad-tempered
fellow, who delighted in causing trouble.

'Is there any work here that I can do?' the youngest
daughter asked.

'Our master doesn't want beggars working for him,' the
scullion answered scornfully. 'Off with you at once before
I set the dogs on you.'

'Who is that?' the housekeeper called out, coming into
the kitchen at that very moment.

'A beggar girl, with dirty hands and face, and a cloak
and cap o' rushes,' the scullion answered. 'The cheek of it!
But I soon sent her on her way, I can tell you.'

'You take too much on yourself,' the housekeeper cried
angrily. 'Call her back at once.'

Scowling, the scullion did as he was bid, and the youngest
daughter came back and stepped into the warm kitchen.

'Well?' said the housekeeper.

'Is there any work here that I can do?' the youngest
daughter asked.

'That depends,' the housekeeper replied. 'Can you rub
and scrub and scour and scrape?'

I can learn, the youngest daughter thought, and she
nodded her head although she had never done any of these
things in her life before.

'Can you wash and bleach and smooth and iron?' the housekeeper asked.

I can learn, the youngest daughter thought, and she
nodded her head although she had never done any of these
things in her life before.

'Can you stir and mix and knead and bake?' the housekeeper asked.

I can learn, the youngest daughter thought, and nodded
her head, although the only food that she knew how to
prepare was a basin of hot gruel.

'I think we can find a use for you,' the housekeeper said.
'Sit down and have some breakfast, and then you can scrub
the kitchen floor.'

When the other servants saw the youngest daughter's dirty
hands and face, and her strange clothes, they laughed and
made jokes about her, and called her Cap o' Rushes: they
gave her all the hard and tiring jobs which they disliked,
but never once did she complain, and never once did she
stop working until the job was properly done.

From first thing in the morning until last thing at night
Cap o' Rushes worked, and then, candle in hand, she crept
up the servants' staircase to the big attic which she shared
with the dairymaid, and first and second kitchen-maids and
the cook.

She had not been there very long before the lord who
owned the mansion announced that he was going to give a
ball for his son. To get the mansion ready and the food
prepared, all the servants worked twice as hard as usual,
and so pleased was the housekeeper when the last prepara-
tions were finished that she told the servants they might
watch the dancing from the minstrels' gallery, provided
that they washed themselves and put on their Sunday
clothes.

'Hurry up and get ready, Cap o' Rushes,' cried the dairymaid, as she and the milkmaid, the first and second kitchen-
maids and the cook washed their faces, took off their working
clothes and put on their Sunday dresses.

'I'm too tired to go and watch the dancing,' Cap o' Rushes
answered, climbing into bed and pulling her rush cloak
about her. 'I'm going to sleep. Don't waken me when you
come back.'

As soon as the others had gone, however, she got up,
took off her cap and cloak, washed herself and her long,
yellow hair, and put on the satin gown which she had
wrapped in the cloak the little maid had given her.

Downstairs she hurried, and when she appeared in the
ballroom, everyone stopped dancing to look at her and

exclaim over her pale gold hair, and her gown of white satin, embroidered with gold and sewn with sapphires as blue as her eyes.

'She is the most beautiful girl in the room,' said the lord's son. Stepping forward with a bow, he asked her to dance and before the first dance was finished, he had fallen head over heels in love with his unknown partner.

All evening they danced together, but just before the ball ended Cap o' Rushes slipped out of the ballroom and hurried upstairs to the attic. Quickly she took off her satin gown and wrapped it in the little maid's cloak; quickly she dirtied her face and her hands and her hair and donned her cloak and cap of rushes, and when the others returned, she was sound asleep in her bed.

'Oh, Cap o' Rushes, you should have been at the ball last night,' the scullion said the following morning. 'You would have been green with envy if you'd seen the beautiful lady who was there. The young lord danced with her the whole of the evening.'

'I wonder who she is,' the dairymaid said.

'And where she comes from,' the milkmaid added.

'Obviously she's a princess,' the cook remarked.

'A *foreign* princess,' the scullion said, pretending that he knew all about princesses.

Cap o' Rushes sighed, as though regretting that she had not been at the ball, and no one knew that it was a sigh of love for the handsome young lord with whom she had danced all the previous evening.

'What is this?' the housekeeper exclaimed, bustling into the kitchen. 'Gossiping at this time of the morning, and not a stroke of work done when the lord has decided to give a second ball for his son tonight.'

'Tonight?' cried the milkmaid and the dairymaid, the first and second kitchen-maids and the cook, all together.

'It's all on account of that foreign princess, I dare say,' said the scullion.

All day the servants worked, and in the evening they

washed and changed before going down to watch the dancing from the minstrels' gallery.

'I'm too tired to watch the dancing,' Cap o' Rushes said, climbing into her bed and pulling her rush cloak about her. 'I'm going to sleep. Don't waken me when you come back.'

As soon as the others had gone, however, she got up, took off her cap and cloak, washed herself and her long, yellow hair, and put on her satin gown.

Downstairs she hurried, and when she appeared in the ballroom, everyone stopped dancing to look at her and admire the pale gold of her hair, her gown of white satin embroidered with gold and sewn with sapphires, and the slow, sweet smile which lit up her face.

'She is the most beautiful girl in the whole country,' said the young lord. Stepping forward with a bow, he asked her to dance with him, and before the first dance was finished, he knew that the only thing which mattered was that she should become betrothed to him.

All evening they danced together, but just before the ball ended, and when no one was looking, Cap o' Rushes slipped out of the ballroom and hurried upstairs to the attic, and when the others returned, she was sound asleep in bed, wrapped in her cap and cloak of rushes.

'Oh, Cap o' Rushes, you should have been at the ball last night,' the scullion said, the next morning. 'You would have been green with envy if you'd seen the foreign princess looking even more beautiful than before, and the young lord dancing with her the whole evening.'

'It's obvious that he's fallen in love with her,' said the dairymaid.

'But still no one knows who she is or where she comes from,' added the milkmaid.

And Cap o' Rushes sighed, as though regretting that she had not been at the ball, and no one knew that it was a sigh of love for the handsome young lord with whom she had danced all the previous evening.

'What is this?' the housekeeper exclaimed, bustling into the kitchen. 'Gossiping at this time of the morning, and not a stroke of work done when the lord has decided to give a third ball for his son tonight.'

'Tonight!' cried the milkmaid and the dairymaid, the first and second kitchen-maids and the cook, all together.

'It's all on account of that foreign princess,' said the scullion.

All day the servants worked, and in the evening, when they had gone to watch the ball from the minstrels' gallery, for the third time Cap o' Rushes washed herself, put on her white satin gown and went down to the ballroom where the young lord awaited her eagerly.

'You are the most beautiful girl in the whole world,' he said as they danced together, and just before the last dance he slipped on her finger a betrothal ring of gold, set with sapphires as blue as her eyes.

'Promise you will marry me soon,' he whispered.

'But you know nothing about me,' Cap o' Rushes protested.

'I know enough. I know that I love you and that if I don't see you again, I shall surely die.'

Just then someone came up to speak to him, and while his attention was distracted, Cap o' Rushes slipped away, so that when the other maids climbed up to the attic, she was sound asleep in her bed.

'Oh, Cap o' Rushes, you should have been at the ball last night,' the scullion said the next morning. 'You would have been green with envy. The beautiful foreign princess was there again, and the young lord danced with her all evening.'

'And then he announced that he is going to marry her,' cried the dairymaid excitedly.

'But first he has to find her,' the milkmaid pointed out.

'That's true,' the first kitchen-maid agreed. 'Each night she has disappeared before the ball was over –'

'– and no one knows where she goes –' added the second kitchen-maid.

'– or what she is called,' finished the cook.

'I know more than you,' boasted the scullion. 'Today the young lord is going out with all his friends and servants to see if he can find his princess. Everyone says that she can't be staying far from here if she could come to the ball every evening.'

Day after day the young lord scoured the countryside, calling first at all the mansions and big houses, and then at all the not-so-big houses, and finally at the cottages and hovels, but no one had seen or heard of the beautiful princess with pale gold hair the colour of the primrose when first it appears in springtime, and eyes as blue as the speedwell.

Day after day the young lord grew paler and thinner and more and more unhappy as he mourned the love he had lost, until at last he was so weak that he could no longer ride forth to look for her, but had to take to his bed. There he lay, sorrowing and sighing, and refusing to eat or drink in spite of all the tempting dishes the cook brought up from the kitchen.

'My son will die of love unless someone can persuade him to eat something,' the old lord cried, coming into the kitchen one morning and wringing his hands in despair.

'I have tried every dish I know,' the cook pleaded.

'Why don't you offer him some gruel?' Cap o' Rushes asked. 'I've heard it said that it is just the thing for a young man who is dying of love.'

'Gruel!' cried the old lord, brightening immediately. 'Why didn't *you* think of that?' he demanded, turning to the cook. 'Make it at once.' And he hurried out of the kitchen and went upstairs to tell his son.

'Gruel?' said the cook. 'It's rather a long time since I made gruel. Perhaps you would like to show me how it's done – just to remind me, of course.'

'Of course,' said Cap o' Rushes.

(And in case you want to know how she knew the way to make gruel – why! she had watched her old nurse make it for supper many a night, and had lent a helping hand, too.)

First she chopped an onion very finely and fried it in suet; then she added salt and pepper, cinnamon and fine oatmeal, and then, stirring all the time, she poured on fresh milk, which the dairymaid had just brought in, and cooked it all gently over the fire.

'There you are,' she said, pouring the gruel into a hot bowl and wrapping a napkin round it – and when no one was looking, she dropped into the bowl the ring which the young lord had given her.

Carrying the gruel carefully, the cook hurried upstairs to where the young lord lay, pale and dying for love of the unknown princess with whom he had danced three nights in succession.

'That smells good,' he said, lifting up his head a fraction of an inch. 'I'll try one spoonful of it.'

When he had tried one spoonful, he smacked his lips and tried another ... and another ... and another, until he came at last to the bottom of the bowl.

And found the ring.

'Where did this come from?' he cried excitedly, sitting up in bed.

'It must belong to the cook,' the old lord said.

'Tell her to come back at once,' the young lord cried.

'Oh, dear! Was there something wrong with the gruel?' the cook asked, panting – because this was the second time that morning she had run up the stairs, and she wasn't as young as she once was, and she was a great deal fatter than she once had been.

'Nothing was wrong with it,' the young lord answered. 'As a matter of fact, it was the best gruel I've ever tasted in my life.'

'Thank you, your lordship,' the cook said. 'I always do my best to please.'

'You pleased better than you know,' said the young lord. 'Now tell me where you got this ring.'

When the cook saw the sapphires sparkling in the sunlight, she had to confess that she knew nothing about the ring because it was not she who had made the gruel, but the new maid, Cap o' Rushes.

'Bring the girl up here,' ordered the young lord, and downstairs the cook ran, seized Cap o' Rushes by the hand and hurried her upstairs, followed by the milkmaid and the dairymaid, the first and second kitchen-maids, the scullion and the housekeeper, who all wanted to know what was going on.

'What do you know about this ring?' the young lord asked, when Cap o' Rushes stood before him.

'I expect she found it somewhere,' said the housekeeper.

'She stole it,' said the scullion spitefully.

But the milkmaid and dairymaid, the first and second kitchen-maids and the cook all shook their heads and cried:

'Oh, no. Cap o' Rushes would never do anything like that.'

(Because, you see, they'd all grown very fond of her – all except the scullion, who was a mean, bad-tempered fellow who could never grow fond of anyone.)

'If you didn't steal it, and you didn't find it, how did you come by it?' the young lord asked.

'It was given to me,' Cap o' Rushes answered. Taking the ring from the young lord, she slipped it on her finger, and then throwing off her cape and hood, she stood there in her white satin dress embroidered with gold and sewn with sapphires, and the sunlight shone on the pale gold of her hair.

'Cap o' Rushes is my betrothed,' the young lord cried, springing out of bed, now completely cured.

'We shall celebrate the wedding next week,' the old lord announced. 'We shall invite everyone in the neighbourhood to a magnificent feast of boar's head, roast suckling pig, baked venison tart, chitterlings, Norfolk dumplings and marrow bones.'

'And gruel,' said the young lord.

'And gruel,' his father agreed.

Naturally, Cap o' Rushes invited her father to the marriage feast.

(She would have invited her two elder sisters, but they had found themselves husbands in the meantime and had run off, without a word to anyone, but with all their father's money.)

The night before the feast Cap o' Rushes went down to the kitchen and told the cook that each dish was to be prepared twice – once with salt and once without – and the cook did as she was told, although she couldn't understand the reason for this strange order.

The next day, when the guests arrived, Cap o' Rushes welcomed her father and pretended not to notice how coldly he spoke to her. Everyone was hungry because they'd travelled a long way to the wedding, and they were delighted at the sight of all the appetizing dishes on the long table. But it was a different matter when they began to eat. Then they discovered that everything – the boar's head, roast suckling pig, baked venison tart, chitterlings, Norfolk dumplings, marrow bones and the gruel – everything had been cooked without salt, and was so tasteless that no one could eat more than a single mouthful.

'What is the meaning of this?' the guests cried angrily. 'You bid us to a wedding feast, and then insult us by offering us unsalted meat which is so tasteless that we can't eat it.'

At this, Cap o' Rushes' father got to his feet and came to the top of the table where his daughter was seated, and kissed her remorsefully.

'Sit down and listen to me,' he said to the guests. 'Hear how foolish a father can be. Once I brought home presents for my daughters, and in my pride I asked them how much they loved me.

'The eldest said she loved me as much as her life: but the next day she left me and took with her half my fortune.

'The second said she loved me better than the whole world, but two days later she stole away with the rest of my fortune.

'Alas! When my youngest daughter said that she loved me as fresh meat loves salt, I did not understand that she loved me best of all.'

'All's well that ends well,' said Cap o' Rushes, and she kissed her father and signalled to the servants to bring in the second meal which had been prepared, and in which all the dishes had been seasoned with salt.

Joyfully each guest ate as much as he could – and some ate more than that – and everyone declared that it was the finest marriage feast they had ever attended.

Because the two older sisters had stolen all their father's money, Cap o' Rushes invited him to come and live at the mansion with her and her husband. Every afternoon he and the old lord went fishing together on the banks of the grey-green river, and every evening they smoked their pipes and played dominoes or chess, and because everyone loved everyone else as fresh meat loves salt, they all lived happily ever after.

2

THE OLD WOMAN AND THE
VINEGAR BOTTLE

Once upon a time there was an old woman who lived in a vinegar bottle by the shores of a cold, grey sea.

Day after day she grumbled and sighed, 'Oh, dearie me! Oh, misery me! Oh, lackaday, lackaday, lackaday me!'

No one paid any attention to her until one fine morning when a good-natured fairy happened to pass that way.

'What is the matter?' the fairy asked. 'Why do you grumble and sigh and look so sad?'

'You'd sigh and look sad if you had to live in a vinegar bottle,' the old woman answered. 'Oh, how happy I'd be if only I had a little thatched cottage, with smoke coming out of the chimney, and a red geranium in a pot in the window.'

'I'm sure I can help you,' the fairy said, smiling happily. 'Now, listen carefully. Wait until the clock in the nearby village has finished striking at midnight, then close your eyes and count up to twenty-seven. Curtsey to the full moon, and when you open your eyes you shall see what you shall see.'

And off she flew.

The old woman waited with what patience she could muster until midnight, and then did as she was bid.

When she opened her eyes the vinegar bottle had vanished, and in its place stood a thatched cottage, with smoke coming out of the chimney and a big red geranium in a pot in the window.

'That's more like the kind of house I should have,' the old woman cried, and she hurried in and shut the door behind her.

Now the fairy was very busy doing this and that and that

and this, so that a whole month passed before she thought
again of the old woman.

'How happy she must be in her cottage,' the fairy said to
herself. 'I think I'll just call and see her.'

Off she flew, but when she arrived at the front door there
sat the old woman, grumbling and sighing, 'Oh, dearie me!
Oh, misery me! Oh, lackaday, lackaday, lackaday me!'

'What is the matter now?' the fairy asked in surprise.
'Why do you grumble and sigh and look so forlorn?'

'You'd sigh and look forlorn if you had to live in a poky
cottage,' the old woman answered crossly. 'Can't you see what
a superior person I've become? I ought to live in a big house
with twelve windows, and a big garden in front full of
yellow sunflowers and blue forget-me-nots. And I should
have twelve servants to come running every time I clap my
hands.'

'I think I can manage that,' the fairy said, after a moment's
hesitation. 'Now listen carefully. Wait until the clock in the
village has finished striking at midnight, then close your eyes
and count up to twenty-seven. Curtsey to the moon, and
when you open your eyes, you shall see what you shall see.'

And off she flew.

'I don't see why I have to wait until midnight,' the old
woman grumbled, but she did as she was bid and when she
opened her eyes the cottage had vanished, and in its place
stood a big house with twelve windows. 'That's more like it,'
she cried, and she hurried through the garden, which was
full of yellow sunflowers and blue forget-me-nots. As soon as
she opened the front door, she clapped her hands, and immediately twelve servants came running to see what she wanted.

Now the fairy was busier than ever, doing this and that
and that and this, so that a whole year passed before she
thought again of the old woman.

'How happy she must be in her big house,' the fairy
thought. 'I think I'll just call and see her.'

Off she flew, but when she arrived at the front door there
sat the old woman, grumbling and sighing, 'Oh, dearie me!

Oh, misery me! Oh, lackaday, lackaday, lackaday me!'

'What is the matter now?' the fairy asked. 'Why do you grumble and sigh and look so miserable?'

'You'd sigh and look miserable if you had to live all by yourself in an ugly house like mine,' the old woman replied crossly. 'Can't you see how grand I've become? I ought to be a duchess and dress in pink satin. I want to live in a fine mansion and have a hundred servants to wait on me, and I want a carriage and six horses so that I can visit my rich friends.'

'I dare say I can manage that,' the fairy said thoughtfully. 'Wait until the clock has finished striking at midnight, then close your eyes and count up to twenty-seven. Curtsey to the moon and when you open your eyes you shall see what you shall see.'

When the old woman opened her eyes, she wasn't at all surprised to find that she had indeed become a duchess dressed in pink satin, while in place of her previous house there now stood a fine mansion. 'That's more like it,' she cried, and she hurried past the carriage and six horses and opened the front door, and in the hall the hundred servants bowed to her.

Now the fairy had so much to do here and there and there and here that three long years passed before she thought of the old woman.

'Surely she must be happy now,' the fairy thought. 'I think I'll just call and see her.'

But when she arrived at the front door the old woman, dressed in pink satin, was waiting for her.

'And about time too,' she snapped. 'Can't you see how important I've become? I've decided that I ought to be the queen and live in a palace. I want to wear a golden crown and sit on a golden throne.'

'Can't you remember what to do?' the fairy asked quietly.

'Of course I can,' the old woman answered scornfully.

'Then do it carefully and you shall see what you shall see.'

Sighing and grumbling, the old woman waited till midnight and did as she was bid.

But when she opened her eyes, mansion, carriage and horses, pink satin gown – all had gone, and she was back inside her vinegar bottle again. And there she remained, because no matter how much the fairy had given her, she had always grumbled and asked for more.

3

SIMON AND THE LITTLE GREEN MAN

In the rich and prosperous county of Northamptonshire there once dwelt a wealthy farmer and his wife: they worked hard themselves from morning until night and they expected those whom they employed to work hard too.

Knowing that the Little People could make bad enemies, the Farmer's wife saw that her maids always left a bowl of water on the hearth last thing at night so that the Little People could wash themselves, and a jug of milk in the dairy for them to drink, and the Farmer saw that his men always left a tiny bundle of kindling after they had chopped the firewood and a few sheaves of corn when they had finished threshing.

One fine spring day the Farmer called together all the men and women and the youths and maids who worked on the farm and in the farmhouse.

'My wife and I are going away for three days,' he said. 'The farmwork must go on and the house must be cared for and so I shall give each of you work to occupy you during our absence. There is, however, one thing which I want you all to remember. Leave the usual gifts for the Little People, but have nothing whatsoever to do with them, for they are cunning and spiteful and delight in causing trouble, and they always get the best of any bargain they make.'

'Yes, Gaffer,' the men said, touching their forelocks and making up their minds to hurry in the opposite direction if they so much as caught a glimpse of a fairy or a goblin, and at the same time they resolved to work just as hard as they did when the Farmer was at home.

'Yes, Gaffer,' the women said, curtseying and making up their minds to clap their hands over their ears at the first whisper of fairy music, and at the same time they resolved that the Farmer's wife should have no cause to complain about their work when she returned.

'As for you, Simon,' the Farmer said, turning to the youngest lad whom he had hired less than a year previously at Boughton Green Fair, 'when you have finished chopping the firewood, I want you to go across to Clem Vengeance by the Red Fox Spinney: that field is the worst pasture on the whole of my farm and this year I am determined to do something about it. Gather up all the stones and pile them in one corner, so that later Tom can take his team there and plough the ground.'

'Yes, Gaffer,' Simon said, touching his forelock and wishing he had been given a more interesting job than gathering stones far away from everyone else in Clem Vengeance; and because he was very young, the thought passed through his mind how pleasant it would have been if the Farmer had forgotten about him altogether and he'd not been given a job at all.

Satisfied that all would be well in their absence, the Farmer and his wife set off on horseback, and Simon, seeing how hard everyone was working, applied himself to chopping and stacking the firewood, so that by tea-time the job was finished and the usual little bundle was waiting for the Little People to collect during the night.

'Off with you to Clem Vengeance,' Tom the foreman ordered, once he had satisfied himself that Simon had chopped all the wood and stacked it neatly. 'If you hurry you'll get several hours' work done before it grows dark.'

Simon nodded his head and set off along the track which led through the village and across the stream and up the far hill to the barren field on the top; he was just drawing near the village when he heard the shouts and laughter of children and young men and girls at play, and as he reached the green he saw there all the young people of the village holding hands and singing as they danced round Dickon, the baker's son, and flaxen-haired Sally, his sister.

> Does you or I or anyone know
> Where oats and beans and barley grow?

they sang, and then they stopped dancing and let go of one another's hands.

> The farmer comes and sows the seed,
> Then he stands and takes his ease,
> Stamps his foot and claps his hand,
> And turns him round to view the land.

And in turn they stamped their feet, clapped their hands and turned round before joining hands again and singing as they circled Dickon and Sally:

> Waiting for a partner,
> Waiting for a partner,
> Open the ring and take me in,
> Make haste and choose your partner.

Dickon pointed to brown-eyed Amy, the shoe-maker's youngest daughter, and she left the ring with a laugh to join him in the centre; but Sally was harder to please, and three times she scanned the boys in the ring, frowning and shaking her head; and then she saw Simon standing to one side, watching, and she smiled and pointed to him and Simon forgot about Clem Vengeance and the stones that were to be gathered up and piled in one corner, and he ran forward and broke through the ring to join Sally in the middle.

> Now you're married you must obey,
> Must be true to all you say,
> Must be kind and very good
> And help your wife to chop the wood,

everyone sang as they whirled round the two couples, dancing faster and faster and laughing with merriment.

'And I shall be very good at chopping wood,' Simon whispered to Sally, 'because that's what I've been doing all day.' And he kissed her on the cheek and watched as she and Dickon ran to join the dancing ring and he was left in the middle with brown-eyed Amy, and the game started once more.

When they tired of 'Choosing Partners', they turned to skipping games, and Sally's flaxen curls bobbed up and down as she jumped higher or quicker or longer than any of the other girls; and when they changed to races, Simon always ran faster than any of the other boys, even though some of them were older and taller than he.

At length, however, it began to grow dark, and the fathers and mothers who had been sitting outside their cottages gossiping and watching the young people enjoy themselves, called out that it was time to be abed, and Simon, suddenly discovering how tired he was, ran back to the farm, ate his supper hungrily, and climbed up to the attic, where he fell asleep as though worn out by a long and hard day's work.

The next morning, full of good resolutions to work extra hard so as to make up for the previous evening's play, Simon set off again for Clem Vengeance, but as he reached the village he saw Sally and Dickon and Amy waiting for him.

'Will you come fishing with us down by the mill?' Sally asked, whereupon Simon immediately forgot about Clem Vengeance and the stones that were to be gathered up and piled in one corner, and off he went with Sally and Dickon and Amy; and they fished by the mill and caught nothing, and they laughed and talked and watched the mayflies spinning and dancing above the water, and in the evening they hurried back to the village green to dance and sing with the others:

> Does you or I or anyone know
> Where oats and beans and barley grow?
> The farmer comes and sows the seed,
> Then he stands and takes his ease,
> Stamps his foot and claps his hand,
> And turns him round to view the land.

Every time Sally was in the middle, she chose Simon as her partner, and Simon in turn would have chosen Sally had not the other girls called out that it wasn't fair and that they wanted a turn too.

At length it began to grow dark, and it was soon time for everyone to be in bed, so, bidding Sally good-night, Simon ran back to the farm, ate his supper hungrily, then climbed up to the attic, where he fell fast asleep as though worn out by a long and hard day's work.

The next morning, full of good resolutions to work even harder than he had meant to work the previous day, Simon set off again for Clem Vengeance, but again, as he reached the village, he saw Sally and Dickon and Amy waiting for him.

'Will you come with us to the woods to gather wild flowers?' Sally asked; whereupon Simon immediately forgot about Clem Vengeance and the stones that were to be gathered up and piled in one corner, and off he went with Sally and Dickon and Amy to the woods where they gathered long-stemmed bluebells, and yellow cowslips, and pale primroses and frail wood anemones; and they made one another crowns and necklaces of daisies, and held yellow buttercups under one another's chins to see who liked butter; and in the evening they hurried back to the village green to dance and sing with the others:

> Waiting for a partner,
> Waiting for a partner,
> Open the ring and take me in,
> Make haste and choose your partner.
>
> Now you're married you must obey,
> Must be true to all you say,
> Must be kind and very good
> And help your wife to chop the wood.

Every time Simon was in the middle, he chose Sally as his partner, and Sally in turn would have chosen Simon had not the other boys called out that it wasn't fair and that they wanted a turn too.

When they tired of 'Choosing Partners', they turned first to skipping games, and Sally jumped higher or quicker or longer than any of the other girls, and then they changed to races and again Simon ran faster than anyone in the village.

At length it began to grow dark and time for everyone to be abed, and bidding Sally good-night, Simon ran back to the farm, ate his supper hungrily, and climbed up to the attic, where he fell fast asleep as though worn out by a long and hard day's work.

When he awoke the next morning, he suddenly realized that some time during the day the Farmer would be returning and that he would find no work at all had been done up on Clem Vengeance.

'Oh, dear!' he cried, springing out of bed, and without even waiting for breakfast he ran along the track to the village, shaking his head as Sally called out to him to join her and Dickon and Amy again that day; over the little hump-backed bridge he ran and up the far hill and at last, quite out of breath, he stopped beside the stile by Red Fox Spinney which led into the barren field.

'Oh, dear!' he cried, climbing over the stile and picking his way slowly across the boulders and stones which were strewn so thickly over the field that it was impossible to make out the colour of the soil below.

'Oh, dear!' he cried, looking down at the tough thistles and the dark green stinging nettles which were the only plants to force their way through the stones. 'I shall never clear away all these stones today. Whatever shall I do? The Gaffer will be so angry with me for playing and singing and dancing when I should have been working.'

'What's the matter, my boy?' a hoarse voice asked. Simon looked all round in surprise, and then he saw a little man dressed in green, with a long white beard, sitting cross-legged on a large boulder and staring at him with round green eyes which never blinked.

'Cat got your tongue?' the goblin asked as Simon stared at him in amazement.

'No,' Simon answered at last. 'It's just that I was surprised. I didn't see you come here.'

'No one ever sees me come anywhere. Or go, either,' the Little Green Man answered sharply. 'And you haven't answered my question. What's the matter?'

'I haven't done my work,' Simon answered slowly, 'and the Gaffer returns this afternoon.' He was so upset at the thought of the trouble he was in that he had quite forgotten how the Farmer had warned them to have nothing to do with the Little People who were cunning and spiteful, and delighted in causing trouble, and always got the best of any bargain they made.

'This afternoon?' The Little Green Man gave a mocking laugh and his beard wagged to and fro. 'Whatever are you worrying about? Why, even if it was this morning, I could still do the work for you.'

'Could you?' Simon asked incredulously. He knew that the Little People were fast workers when they liked, but he didn't believe one of them could work fast enough to gather up all the stones and pile them in a corner that morning.

'Of course I could,' the Little Green Man shouted, dancing up and down with rage on the boulder because he could see that Simon didn't believe him. 'I'll tell you what I'll do. I'll make a bargain with you. Can you run?'

'I'm the best runner in Northamptonshire,' Simon said, exaggerating a little to impress the Little Green Man.

'Then let me see how quickly you can run back to that stile,' the Little Green Man said, 'and if I do your work and catch you before you're there, then you must come back with me and work for me for seven years without any wages.'

'Simon! Simon!' a voice called out, and Simon looked across the field to see Sally standing on the far side of the stile. 'Simon, don't listen to him. No matter what trouble you're in, don't listen to him. Come here and I'll help you somehow. Please come here.'

'Go to her if you want,' the Little Green Man jeered. 'But well you know that *I'm* the only one that can help you.'

Simon shivered. He knew that what the Little Green Man said was true; but he also knew that one Fairy year equalled seven mortal years, and that if he did not run fast enough to reach the stile before all the stones were gathered and piled in the corner, by the time he finished working for the Little Green Man and returned to earth Sally and all his friends would be tired and old. Then he laughed. No one could possibly do the work in less time than it would take him to run to the stile.

'Right!' he shouted, and he began to run as fast as he could over the uneven, stony ground.

'Right!' shouted the Little Green Man, and he stamped his foot and immediately the stones and boulders began to rise in the air and fly into the far corner of the field.

'Faster, faster!' Sally cried, wringing her hands as Simon raced towards her, bent low to avoid the flying stones which whipped through the air dangerously close to his unprotected head.

'Faster, faster!' she cried as the last stone fell on the huge pile in the corner of the field and the Little Green Man laughed in malicious triumph.

'Faster, oh faster!' she whispered, biting her knuckles as the Little Green Man swished across the field as though borne by the wind, his skinny hand outstretched to claim his un-willing servant.

But Simon, hearing the malicious laughter and the swish of the wind as the Little Green Man raced up behind him, put on a last, desperate burst of speed, sprang high in the air and landed safely on the far side of the stile beside Sally.

Furiously the Little Green Man glared at the breathless Simon, the rejoicing Sally, and then with a loud cry of rage he disappeared, and all was still and quiet and peaceful.

'I got the best of him,' Simon gasped. 'He didn't know I could run so fast.'

Sally shook her flaxen curls.

'Don't be too sure,' she said. 'The Little People are cunning and spiteful and they always get the best of any bargain they make. Promise me you'll never have anything to do with any of them again.'

Simon was only too pleased to promise this because he knew how nearly the Little Green Man had caught him; and then, hand in hand, they walked down the hill and over the bridge and back to the village.

That evening the Farmer and his wife returned, and immediately the Gaffer went round the farm, well pleased to see how much work had been done during his absence: but when he climbed the steep hill to Clem Vengeance, he rubbed his eyes at the sight of the mountain of stones in the far corner, the good brown soil revealed in what had hitherto been a barren field.

'Once we plough up those thistles and nettles and sow with grass seed, this'll be the best pasture of the lot and we'll have to change its name from Clem Vengeance,' the Farmer thought. 'But Simon must have worked day and night to clear away all those stones. I didn't know the lad had it in him. Tomorrow I'll give him a silver shilling and a whole day's holiday and he can go off to the fair in Northampton and enjoy himself.'

Well pleased, Simon took the silver shilling and the following day he went to the fair with Dickon and Sally and Amy, and they laughed at the Punch and Judy show, and marvelled at the acrobats and jugglers, and gasped at the man who ate fire; and they ate gilt gingerbreadmen and Simon bought Sally a blue ribbon to match her eyes, and in the evening they returned to the village to dance on the green.

Scarcely had they begun to sing than the Farmer appeared and stamped his foot and roared out:

'Simon! Follow me!'

Without another word the Farmer strode off down to the stream and over the little hump-backed bridge and up the steep hillside; and Simon followed behind, sometimes walking and sometimes running to keep up with the pace set by the Gaffer, and wondering all the time what was the matter; and the boys and girls who had been dancing followed Simon, whispering and laughing and asking Sally if she had any idea what it was all about; and the parents followed their children because if something was going to happen, they didn't want to miss it.

At length the Farmer got to the stile leading to Clem Vengeance, and there he stopped. And Simon stopped behind him. And Sally and the boys and girls stopped behind Simon. And the parents stopped behind them. And everyone looked at Clem Vengeance.

'Oh, dear!' Simon said, biting his lip and sighing, because the field was just as it had been when the Farmer went away, with the boulders and stones strewn so thickly over it that it was impossible to make out the colour of the soil below.

'You were right,' he said, turning to Sally. 'You said the Little People always get the best of any bargain they make.'

Because there was nothing else he could do, he told the Farmer how he had enjoyed himself instead of working, and how the Little Green Man had offered to do his work and then had tricked him when he found Simon could run faster than he imagined.

'Ah, well! You've learned your lesson the hard way,' the Farmer said. 'You'll know better than to trust one of the Little People again. And when are you going to start clearing this field?'

'Now, if you want,' Simon offered.

'I'll help him,' Sally said, stepping forward and looking up proudly at Simon.

'So will we,' said Dickon and Amy.

'Time enough for that on Monday,' the Farmer said. 'Saturday night is for dancing on the village green.'

Everyone cheered and laughed and back they all hurried to the village green and this time everyone joined in the dance, young and old, parents and children and even the

grandparents; and the Farmer and his wife laughed as they
sang:

> Does you or I or anyone know
> Where oats and beans and barley grow?
> The farmer comes and sows the seed,
> Then he stands and takes his ease,
> Stamps his foot and claps his hand
> And turns him round to view the land.

'Stands and takes his ease, indeed!' said the Farmer
indignantly. 'There's a lot more to farming than that, and I
don't mean getting Little Green Men to help you.'

But he joined in the dance all the same, and he laughed
and winked one eye and sang louder than anyone:

> Now you're married you must obey,
> Must be true to all you say,
> Must be kind and very good
> And help your wife to chop the wood.

4

THE TAILOR'S APPRENTICE
AND THE WIFE OF DELORAINE

Not so very long ago it was the custom of master tailors in most of the towns in the Lowlands of Scotland to leave their workshops at certain times of the year, and, with their workmen and apprentices, to journey to the remote country houses and farms, altering and repairing old suits and dresses, measuring and making new ones.

Because they frequently had to travel long distances on horseback, the men had to rise very early, often before daybreak. This meant that when they arrived at their destination for the day, they were ready for a good meal before they started their work.

Some farmers' wives were more generous than others in the fare that they offered the tailors, and naturally the men were always eager to go to those places where the food was appetizing and the helpings generous.

There was one farm in particular where, year in and year out, the tailors were sure of having such a generous breakfast that it would set them up for the rest of the day, and that was at the farm of Deloraine, in the valley of the Yarrow Water.

If, however, they mentioned the generosity of the farmer's wife at other places which they visited along the Yarrow Water, or in the neighbouring Ettrickdale, they could not help noticing how the women stopped smiling, and looked nervously around before muttering:

'The Wife of Deloraine? We know what we know, and there's no welcome in our houses for her.'

When the tailors asked what the women meant, they shrugged their shoulders and bustled off to see to their household duties, and the tailors, looking at the small helpings of porridge which they had been given and the little jug of skimmed milk, put the remarks down to jealousy.

'It's a pity,' they said, 'that all our customers aren't as clever, or thrifty, or businesslike – or whatever it is – as the Wife of Deloraine.'

Now it happened one fine spring day that the master tailor of Selkirk received a message that the Wife of Deloraine wished to engage him and his men the following Monday, to measure her goodman for a new suit for Whitsuntide, and to make her a gown of the finest wool.

Long before the sun was up on Monday morning, the master tailor's wife had risen, prepared a meal for her husband, his men and his apprentices, and they were all ready to start when she noticed that the youngest apprentice was missing. This lad had two faults in his master's eyes – he was too fond of his bed in the morning and he was far too curious about things which did not concern him. However, as these were faults which the master tailor frequently found in his apprentices, he had little doubt that he would eventually cure him of them.

Up the stairs the master tailor climbed to the attic where the lad slept, to find that it was just as he suspected – the boy had turned over after he was called, gone to sleep again and now was snoring lustily.

Shaking him none too gently, the master tailor stripped off the bedclothes and stood over the lad while he pulled on his breeches and then hurried down to join his companions, without bothering to wash either his hands or his face.

Sleepily the lad mounted his nag and sleepily he jogged along the road, with no eye for the gradually lightening sky, the green hills and the dark moors beyond, and no ear for the song of the Ettrick Water as it flowed through lush meadows and leafy forests.

By the time they had reached the farm of Deloraine, in the valley of the Yarrow Water, the sun had warmed him and the skylark had wakened him with its song, and he had just such an appetite as you would have expected of a growing lad who had ridden many miles without first breaking his fast.

'Good day to you,' the Wife of Deloraine cried, as the master tailor and his craftsmen and apprentices dismounted at the back door and unsaddled their ponies. 'We have just this moment sat down to breakfast. I have laid places for you and there is enough and more than enough for everyone.'

Into the stone-flagged kitchen the tailors hurried, greeted the farmer and his men, and took their places at the table, and the youngest apprentice, as befitting the one who was least important, sat at the bottom, with his back to the door.

Immediately the Wife of Deloraine and her maids plied them with porridge straight from the big iron pot on the fire, and handed round a huge earthenware jug of fresh milk, thick with cream.

'This is what I call porridge,' the youngest apprentice whispered to the second-youngest apprentice. 'It bears no relation to the lumpy, half-cooked oatmeal which the master tailor's wife gives us, which sticks in your throat so that you can only swallow a few spoonfuls, and then, half-an-hour later, you find yourself almost dying of starvation.'

'And this is what I call milk,' the second-youngest apprentice replied. 'It bears no relation to that thin, watered stuff which the master tailor's wife gives us, which has no taste at all, so that even if you drank the whole jug, half-an-hour later you'd find yourself almost dying of thirst.'

Round the table bustled the Wife of Deloraine, encouraging everyone to have second helpings, aye, and a third if he wanted.

'A man cannot do his work properly, whether he be farmer or tailor, with an empty belly,' she declared.

'The jug of milk is nearly empty,' the farmer said to one of the maids. 'Go and fill it up again.'

'I am sorry, master,' the girl answered, 'but there is no more milk in the house.'

'Serve the master tailor with more porridge while I fetch the milk,' the Wife of Deloraine ordered, and picking up a large pail from the shelf at the side of the fireplace, she hurried round the table and out of the back door.

If there's no milk in the house, she must have gone out to milk one of her cows, the youngest apprentice thought, and because he had eaten all that he could possibly eat, and because one of his faults was that he was far too curious about things which did not concern him, he got up very quietly and slipped round the half-open door. Creeping along the stone-flagged passage, he caught a glimpse of the Wife of Deloraine in the empty dairy, and, full of curiosity to know what she was doing, he hid behind a cupboard in a dark corner and watched.

Right through the long room the Wife of Deloraine walked until she came to a wooden peg on the far wall, just beside a little window which gave on to the fertile valley of the Yarrow Water, where the cows cropped the rich, green grass. Holding her pail underneath, she turned the peg clockwise, and immediately, to the lad's amazement, a stream of rich, creamy milk poured out of the wall. When the basin was almost full, she muttered something beneath her breath, turned the peg in the opposite direction, and the flow of milk ceased.

Scarcely daring to breath, the lad pressed himself even deeper into the shadows, and the Wife of Deloraine passed by without seeing him, and returned with her pail of milk to the kitchen. Not long after the lad took his place at the table again, and watched his companions drinking down with evident relish the milk which had flowed so strangely from the twisting of a peg in the dairy wall.

It was all most peculiar, the youngest apprentice thought, and throughout the morning as the tailors sat in the room set apart for them, measuring and cutting, basting and sewing, folding and ironing, he could not get the strange scene out of his head.

Just about midday the master tailor put down his work, adjusted his spectacles, straightened his back and stretched his arms above his head.

'It's warm for the time of the year,' he said. 'For the past hour I've been growing more and more thirsty. I'd give anything for a bowl of that rich milk we had with our porridge this morning.'

'Milk?' the youngest apprentice cried, dropping his box of pins to the ground as he sprang to his feet. He hadn't got used to sitting still for hours on end, sewing until his eyes ached and his fingers were numb. 'Milk? I'll go and get you some.' And he was off before anyone could stop him.

The Wife of Deloraine was not in the kitchen and not in the scullery. She was not in the dining-room and not in the parlour. When he stood on the stairs and called, there was no answer, so she didn't appear to be in any of the bedrooms. He couldn't find her in the yard or in any of the outbuildings, and so he decided he'd manage nicely without her.

Picking up the pail from the shelf beside the kitchen fireplace, he hurried down the passage and into the empty dairy. Along to the far wall he walked, and holding his pail underneath, he turned the wooden peg clockwise, and immediately a stream of rich, creamy milk poured out of the wall.

When the pail was almost full, he tried to turn the peg in the opposite direction. But it refused to move, and the milk kept on pouring out, over the top of the basin, running down the sides, splashing on to the ground and forming an ever widening pool at his feet.

'Help!' he cried in alarm. 'Help me, someone. I'm drowning in milk, and I can't swim. Help, help!'

From their room in the house the master tailor and the workmen and the other apprentices all ran, stopping in the doorway of the dairy to gape at the milk which poured out of the wall and now covered most of the floor.

'Someone must try to stop it. All you have to do is turn this knob,' the youngest apprentice wailed, whereupon the master tailor hurried forward, splashing through the ever deepening milk to push and pull and shove and twist and twirl and turn the wooden peg.

But all to no avail. The milk continued to pour out in a

steady white stream that lapped round their ankles.

One by one the others tried their strength and cunning on the peg, but even when one of the workmen brought his iron, and another the kitchen poker, they could not move it, and the milk continued to pour out in a steady white stream that lapped around their calves.

'We'll all drown if we don't do something quickly,' the master tailor cried. 'Fetch pails and buckets, bowls and jugs, baths and barrels – fetch anything that you can find so that we can collect the milk before it floods the whole house.'

Away they scuttled – tailors and workmen and apprentices – and back they rushed, pushing and shoving, arguing and shouting as they held out whatever receptacle they could find, and the milk poured out relentlessly, filling each dish so that the bearer had to stagger out into the yard with it, put it down, and hurry back to find something else which would take this terrible, never-ending stream of creamy milk.

Just when every single pail and bucket, bowl and jug, bath and barrel, cup and saucer, dish and plate had been filled to the brim and carried out into the yard, and there was nothing at all left for the panic-stricken tailors to place under the steady white stream, the Wife of Deloraine appeared at the door, her eyes flashing and her face as black as thunder.

'You fools!' she screamed. 'You imbeciles. Do you know what you've done? You've milked dry every cow between Ettrickdale and the Yarrow Water, and not a farmer in the district will get so much as a drop of milk today, even if he is dying of thirst. Out of my way, you interfering busybodies.' Pushing them out of the way, she waded across to the far wall, muttered something beneath her breath, turned the peg in an anti-clockwise direction, and at long last the flow of milk stopped.

'That was all your fault,' the master tailor said to the youngest apprentice, as they crept away, collected up their cloth and scissors, needles and thread, canvas and irons, and rode off hastily, back to Selkirk.

'How was I to know that she was a witch, and the milk she gave so freely was stolen from all the farmers of Ettrickdale and the Yarrow Water?' the lad asked. 'You won't catch me going back there, Master. Not for all the gold in Scotland.'

'Perhaps that'll teach you not to be so curious about things which don't concern you,' the master tailor said sharply, resolving at the same time that no one would catch him going back to the farmhouse of Deloraine either.

'It's a mercy she didn't turn the lot of you into frogs or newts or spiders, or something equally unpleasant,' his wife said that evening, when he told her all that had happened.

'So that is what has been happening to our milk,' the farmers of the Yarrow Water and Ettrickdale cried angrily, when they heard the story that the tailors of Selkirk had to tell. 'We always suspected that our cows were bewitched, but now we know for certain. If they don't yield the proper amount in future, the Wife of Deloraine had better look out for herself.'

Whether the Wife of Deloraine heard their threats, or whether she was furious because it was the tailors who had discovered her secret, no one knows, but from that very day the cows of Yarrow Water and Ettrickdale yielded greater quantities than ever before of the richest and creamiest milk in the whole of Scotland.

And something else happened too – and people blamed the tailor's apprentice for this – but after that day, no one who came to work for the Wife of Deloraine was ever offered milk. Oh, no! No matter how far they had ridden, how hungry and thirsty they were, all they were ever given was a very small helping of boiled potatoes and cabbage!

5

THE SMALL-TOOTH DOG

A long, long time ago, in the town of Norton, in Derbyshire, there lived a wealthy merchant who had only one child, a daughter named Anne, whom he loved more than anything else in the world.

Frequently the merchant, accompanied by his servant, had to make long journeys on horseback to buy and sell his goods in distant fairs and markets, and every time he returned to his home in Derbyshire, he would bring with him a present – a length of brocade for a new gown, a lace shawl or a piece of jewellery, a talking parrot or a pet monkey – for his daughter, Anne.

Now it happened that once he and his servant were spurring home late at night, their saddle bags bulging with money after a successful week's trading in London. Normally the merchant arranged his journeys so that he travelled only by daylight, but on this occasion his horse had cast a shoe and he had had great difficulty in finding a smith, and only by offering twice the usual price was he able to persuade the smith to interrupt the work he was doing and shoe his horse.

Another half-hour and we shall be in Norton, the merchant was thinking, when suddenly three highwaymen, masked and armed, sprang out from behind a thick hedge and seized the horses by their bridles. The servant they knocked unconscious and the merchant they dragged from his horse and threw on the ground and then they ripped open the saddle bags.

'Gold and silver!' they cried. 'Enough to keep us in idleness for years!'

Their greedy eyes lit up as they plunged their hands into the money; then they exchanged secret glances, and the merchant knew that now they were planning to get rid of him and his servant so that no one would know what they had done.

'Help!' he cried. 'Help, oh help!'

But in the gathering darkness there were no other travellers to be seen, no one to hear him and come to his aid.

'Take my money, but spare me and my servant,' he begged, but the highwaymen only laughed mockingly and raised their pistols.

'Help!' the merchant cried. 'Help, oh help!'

Just when he had given up all hope a monstrous dog, its eyes green and glaring, leaped over the hedge with a deep-throated bark that echoed and re-echoed in the lonely lane.

The moment the highwaymen saw the creature, they dropped the merchant's money and their pistols and fled, shrieking, and long after the darkness had swallowed them up their terrified voices could be heard in the distance.

'How ever can I thank you?' the merchant said, trying to struggle to his feet, but so badly had the highwaymen treated him that he could not stand.

'Put your master on my back,' said the dog to the servant, who had now recovered consciousness, 'and then climb on yourself, and I will see that you are both cared for.'

The servant did as he was told, and the dog carried the two men along a winding path to a big, stone house; through the front door he took them, up a wide, carved staircase, to a bedroom hung with costly tapestries, and there he bathed their wounds himself, and later unseen hands fed them and soft music lulled them to restful sleep.

To their amazement, the next morning both the merchant and his servant found themselves fit and well.

'I can't believe it,' the merchant exclaimed. 'Last night I had cuts and bruises that would take at least ten days to heal.'

'I could have sworn the villains broke my right arm when I tried to fight them off,' the servant said. 'Yet now I can move it freely and it doesn't even ache.'

'You did have severe cuts and bruises,' said the dog, appear-

ing suddenly. 'And your servant's right arm was broken, but I have healed your injuries and you may continue on your journey whenever you wish.'

'How ever can I thank you?' the merchant said, looking at the monstrous dog with its black, matted coat, its flaring nostrils and huge green eyes, and thinking that never in his life had he seen such an ugly creature. 'You saved my life and my servant's. What can I give you in return?' Quickly he ran over in his mind all his most cherished possessions. 'Would you like the great carp which swims in the pool in my garden and which can speak seven times seven different languages?'

'No, thank you,' said the dog, shaking his ugly head.

Again the merchant ran over in his mind all his most cherished possessions.

'Perhaps you would prefer my goose which lays a golden egg every morning and every evening, and carries it upstairs and places it in the linen coffer on the landing?'

'No, thank you,' said the dog, shaking his ugly head.

Once again the merchant ran over in his mind all his most cherished possessions.

'I know what you would like,' he said at length, 'and I will part with it gladly because you have saved my life. Take my lovely Venetian mirror which reveals the thoughts of anyone to whom you happen to be talking.'

'No, thank you,' said the dog, shaking his ugly head.

'Then what can I give you?' the merchant asked, knowing that he had offered the dog the choicest of his treasures.

'I too have a carp in the pool in my garden,' the dog said, 'but mine speaks seven hundred times seven different languages.

'I too have a goose which lays a golden egg each morning and evening, but mine sits on her eggs and hatches out geese of the purest gold, which in turn lay other golden eggs.

'As for your Venetian mirror which reveals what people are thinking about, my mirror shows me what people have thought in the past and are going to think in the future.

'I have a house and lands and possessions. All I lack is a wife. Give me your daughter, Anne.'

When he heard what the dog wanted the merchant shuddered. His lovely daughter marry this dreadful creature? It was impossible. The dog was surely joking?

But the dog wasn't joking.

In vain the merchant pleaded and argued: in vain he offered his house and garden and all his possessions.

All the dog wanted was Anne.

'Very well,' the merchant said sadly. 'I owe you my life and I must pay the price you demand, even though it breaks my heart.

'How I shall tell my child, I do not know. Give me one week with her, and then you may come and fetch her.'

'One week with her you may have,' the dog agreed, and the merchant set off with his servant, sighing and weeping at what had befallen him.

When Anne heard that her father had promised that she should marry a monstrous black dog, she couldn't believe her ears.

'I won't do it,' she cried, stamping her foot angrily. 'Nothing will make me marry a monstrous, black dog with green eyes.'

She ran upstairs to her room, locked the door and threw herself on her bed, and she set about thinking what she could do – until at last she hit on a plan.

The next day, when she came downstairs, she apologized for losing her temper, was kind and loving and gentle until she was sure that her father could refuse her nothing, and then she tried to coax him into saying that she need not marry the dog.

'I owe the creature my life,' the merchant said sadly, 'and I must pay the price he demands, even though it breaks my heart.'

At this, Anne lost her temper again, stamped her foot angrily and ran upstairs to her room. Locking the door she threw herself on her bed and set about thinking what she could do – until at last she hit on another plan.

The following day, when she came downstairs, she apologized for losing her temper, was kind and loving and gentle until she was sure that her father could refuse her nothing, and then she tried to argue with him and prove that, while a promise given to a person was binding, a promise given to an animal didn't matter.

'Dog or man, it makes no difference,' the merchant said sadly. 'I owe him my life and I must pay the price he demands, even though it breaks my heart.'

When at last the seventh day arrived and Anne realized that nothing would make her father break his word, she put on her oldest clothes, disarranged her hair, and went to the front door where the dog was waiting for her.

'What an ugly creature you are,' she said, scowling with anger.

'Jump on my back,' the dog said, ignoring the scowl, the untidy hair and the old clothes, 'and I will carry home as my bride the most beautiful girl in Derbyshire.'

Anne wanted to stamp her foot and refuse to go, but somehow she found herself sitting on the dog's back, and the next moment it was galloping faster than the wind with her to his house.

'All this is yours,' he said, taking her first through a garden where fountains played among the loveliest and most sweet-smelling flowers.

'And all this is yours,' he said, taking her into the house, where rare carpets from Persia covered the floors, the walls were hung with tapestries from France and choice furniture filled the rooms.

'And all these are yours,' he said, opening a large cupboard and showing her the finest collection of dresses in every conceivable colour, fashioned in every conceivable material and style.

'You cannot see my servants,' he continued, 'but they are all around you to obey your slightest wish. Anything you want, you shall have; but remember this one thing – you must never go farther than the garden wall.

'We shall be married this afternoon and then I must leave you straight after the ceremony as I have work to do.'

Things mightn't be as bad as I feared, Anne thought, as lazy day succeeded lazy day. She now owned a lovely house and garden and all the dresses she could possibly desire; she only had to wish for something, to be given it instantly; and the monstrous black dog was so busy that never once did she set eyes on him after the marriage ceremony. Things mightn't be as bad as I feared, she thought again, as lazy week succeeded lazy week, but they're not as good as I'd hoped. I'm so lonely and I do so miss my father and my own home in Norton.

A sudden wave of homesickness engulfed her and she sat down on an embroidered cushion and began to weep.

'What is the matter?' the dog asked, suddenly appearing in front of her.

'I want to go back home to see my father,' Anne replied, looking up and shuddering as she realized that the black dog was even bigger and uglier than she had remembered.

'I suppose that's understandable,' the dog said. 'If you'll promise to come back after three days, I'll take you to Norton willingly. But, first of all, tell me what you call me.'

Anne looked at the creature and shuddered.

'A monstrous, horrid, small-tooth dog,' she answered.

'In that case, you can't go,' the dog said angrily.

'Oh, please, please let me go,' Anne begged, beginning to cry again – but not too much in case her eyes became red and swollen. 'I didn't mean to hurt your feelings. In fact, I didn't know that dogs had any feelings. Oh, please let me go home to my father.' And she pleaded so prettily that at last the dog relented.

'Very well,' he said. 'But first of all, tell me what you call me.'

'Sweet as a honeycomb,' Anne answered promptly.

'Jump on my back,' the dog commanded. There was a strange look in his huge, green eyes, but Anne was so busy combing her hair that she did not notice it.

On to the dog's back she jumped and away he sped faster than the wind until he came to a wooden stile.

'What did you say that you call me?' he asked, pausing at the stile.

'A monstrous, horrid, small-tooth dog,' Anne replied, thinking that she was nearly home and that there was no need for her to pretend any longer.

'If that's what you think, you can't go home to your father,' the dog said angrily, and he returned to his house with Anne still on his back.

'You have a lovely house and garden, all the dresses you can possibly desire, and you only have to wish for something to be given it instantly. Why aren't you content?' he asked.

'Because I'm lonely,' Anne replied. 'The garden is very lovely, but when I walk in it, I want someone beside me, to talk to me and answer my questions.'

The dog considered this.

'I have a great deal of work to do,' he said, 'but I can spare some time this week.'

And so each morning he walked beside Anne and told her the names of the flowers, bidding her touch this one and smell that one, and he taught her to distinguish between the songs of the birds and to whisper the no-words which were the lullaby of the fountains.

For six days Anne was so interested that she quite forgot how monstrous and ugly the dog was, but when she awakened on the seventh morning she felt sad and homesick, and going downstairs, she sat on her embroidered cushion and began to weep.

'What is the matter?' the dog asked, suddenly appearing in front of her.

'I want to go back home to see my father,' she answered, looking up and shuddering as she saw how monstrous and ugly the creature was.

'I suppose that's understandable,' the dog said. 'If you'll promise to come back after three days, I'll take you to Norton willingly. But first of all, tell me what you call me.'

'Sweet as a honeycomb,' Anne answered promptly.

'Jump on my back,' the dog commanded. Once again there was a strange look in his huge, green eyes, but Anne was so busy smoothing her gown that she did not notice it.

On to the dog's back she jumped and away he sped, faster than the wind, over the stile which they had reached the previous week, and on until he came to a second stile.

'What did you say that you call me?' he asked, stopping suddenly.

'A monstrous, horrid, small-tooth dog,' Anne answered, thinking that as she was nearly home, there was no need for her to pretend any longer.

'If that's what you think, you can't go home to your father,' the dog said angrily, and he returned to his house with Anne still on his back.

'You have a lovely house and garden, all the dresses you can possibly desire, and I have walked by your side each morning and talked to you. Why aren't you content?' the dog asked.

'Because I'm still lonely,' Anne replied. 'The house is very lovely, but when I walk through it, I want someone beside me, to talk to me and answer my questions.'

The dog considered this.

'I have a great deal of work to do,' he said, 'but I can spare some more time this week.'

Each morning he walked beside Anne in the garden, and each afternoon he walked beside her in the house, and he talked about the tapestries of France and the carpets of Persia and the brocade curtains from the Far East, and in the library they looked at the books which contained tales of King Arthur and the Knights of the Round Table, and Robin Hood and his men; and each evening they sat down at a little table and the dog taught Anne to play chess with ivory chessmen which were a hundred times older than she was.

For six days Anne was so interested that she quite forgot how monstrous and ugly the dog was, but when she awakened on the seventh morning, she felt sad and homesick, and going downstairs, she sat on her embroidered cushion and began to weep.

'What is the matter?' the dog asked, suddenly appearing in front of her.

'I want to go back home to see my father,' she answered, looking up and shuddering as she saw how monstrous and ugly the creature was.

'I suppose that's understandable,' the dog said. 'If you'll promise to come back after three days, I'll take you to Norton willingly. But first of all, tell me what you call me.'

'Sweet as a honeycomb,' Anne replied promptly.

'Jump on my back,' the dog commanded. For the third time there was a strange look in his huge, green eyes, but Anne was so busy tying the ribbon in her hair that she did not notice it.

On to the dog's back she jumped and away he sped, faster than the wind, over the stile which they had reached the first week, and over the stile which they had reached the second week, and on until at last they reached the merchant's house in Norton.

'What did you say you called me?' the dog asked, as Anne jumped off his back and ran up the steps to the front door.

She was safe now, Anne thought, grasping the knocker to summon the servants, and she turned round with a triumphant laugh and looked at the dog.

Never in all her life had she seen such a monstrous, horrid, small-tooth creature.

'You know perfectly well what I call you,' she cried scornfully. 'A monstrous –'

She broke off suddenly, for the very first time looking into the dog's green eyes and seeing there the desperate sadness. Now she remembered how he had left her alone until she had asked him to walk beside her; she thought of how he had taught her the names of the flowers and the songs of the birds and the no-words which were the lullaby of the fountains; she recalled how they had talked of tapestries and brocade curtains and carpets, and looked at books and played chess with ivory chessmen a hundred times older than she was.

Suddenly she knew that the dog had been good and kind and patient ever since she had married him, and she knew that it didn't matter to her how monstrous or ugly he was.

Down the steps she ran, to fling her arms round his neck.

'I love you dearly,' she cried, 'and I call you sweeter than a honeycomb.'

Immediately the monstrous, black dog disappeared and in its place stood a handsome young man with dark hair and dark eyes and a smile which revealed small, white, even teeth.

'At last you have said the words which released me from the witch's spell,' he cried. 'She made me so ugly that I despaired of anyone as beautiful as you ever loving me.'

'I didn't want to love you,' Anne admitted, 'but you were so good and kind that I just had to.'

Of course Anne was very pleased to find that she had married not a monstrous, black dog, but an extremely handsome young man; and the merchant was particularly pleased because his son-in-law, as well as being handsome, was immensely wealthy; and so everyone was well satisfied and they all lived together happily ever after.

6

THE LAMBTON WORM

Note: In the North of England the word worm *was used to describe any dragon- or serpent-like creature.*

From the moment he was born, the young heir of Lambton was spoilt.

His nurse spoilt him because he had blue eyes, dimpled cheeks and an entrancing, toothless smile. His parents spoiled him because they had been married a long time and had almost given up hope of having any children. The servants spoiled him because, as he grew up, he took great pleasure in sitting with them in the long winter evenings, listening to their talk of the good old days when his ancestors had first come to dwell on the banks of the River Wear, in County Durham.

By the time he was a young man, he was so used to having his own way, to saying what he liked and doing what he wanted, that it never occurred to him to consider anyone else's feelings.

At an early age, he announced to his parents that he was no longer going to attend church with them on Sunday mornings because the service was so dull and he had better things to do with his time; and, because they wanted their son to be happy, they agreed, rather sadly, that of course he could do whatever he pleased.

Now one Sunday, just as the bell was tolling in the stone church to remind the lord and lady, and all who worked in Lambton Hall that the morning service would begin in a few minutes, the young heir suddenly lost his temper. Since daybreak he had been casting his line into the swiftly flowing river, and he hadn't caught one single fish. Angrily he cursed the weather, the bait, the river and the fish which refused to rise and then, to round things off, he seized his rod and broke it across his knee.

'And what do you think you're doing, standing there, you idle, good-for-nothing?' he cried, turning on the lad who had accompanied him. 'Run back to the Hall as if the devil himself was at your heels and bring me a new rod and fresh bait.'

Terrified, the lad did as he was bid, returning red in the face and breathless, with a new rod and some fresh bait which the cook had found for him.

To the amazement of both the young heir and the lad the very second the line was cast, the bait was taken. But landing the catch was another matter. For nearly an hour, his excitement growing all the time, the young heir played the fish until sweating and exhausted, he finally succeeded in landing the creature on the grassy bank beside him.

'Who would have thought such a little thing could have fought such a long time?' the lad said, drawing back a couple of steps, for he did not like the look of his master's catch.

'I've never seen anything like it before,' the young heir said in disgust, staring down at the ugly, scaly creature, a mere six inches in length, which had caused him so much trouble. He had hoped for a fine roach or perch or even a splendid carp: he would have been quite content with an eel, for the cook was famous for her magnificent eel pies. But an ugly, scaly worm with threshing tail and sharp claws and a malevolent look in its glassy eyes!

'Ugh!' he exclaimed, and picking it up, he tossed it into a nearby well. 'I've had enough fishing for today,' he said to his lad. 'Take my tackle back to the Hall. I'm going for a walk.' And he was just turning away when he saw an old man approaching along the track which ran by the river bank.

'Good morning, Stranger,' he said, because he really was quite a polite young man – except when he lost his temper, of course.

'Good morning, young man,' the stranger answered. 'And

what have you caught this fine Sunday morning?'

'Since you ask me,' the young heir answered, 'I think I've caught the devil himself. Look in the well there and tell me what you think.'

Curiously, the old man peered down the well, shaking his head in amazement.

'Never have I seen such a strange creature in all my three score years and ten,' he said. 'It's neither fish nor lizard nor newt.'

'It's just a very small, very ugly worm,' the young heir remarked casually.

'Perhaps,' the old man agreed. 'But it seems to me that this Sunday catch of yours was sent to make you think.'

'Think?' the young heir said. 'What about?'

'Whether you want to spend the rest of your life fishing for such small, ugly worms,' the old man answered, and he walked on down the river bank, leaving the young heir staring down at the worm and scratching his head perplexedly.

All the rest of the day he sat by the River Wear, lost in thought, looking up guiltily when the church bells rang for the evening service. That night he tossed and turned on his bed, unable to sleep because of the thoughts which troubled him, as he had travelled a long way from the worm he had caught to himself and his behaviour.

Early the next morning, he went to see his parents.

'I have been thinking for nearly twenty-four hours,' he said, 'and I have come to the conclusion that all my life I have been selfish and thoughtless. Now the time has come when I must have a care for others. I have decided to join the Crusaders who are leaving this country in a few weeks' time to liberate the Holy Land from the heathen Turks.'

Naturally his parents wished that he had not chosen to journey so far away from them, but they rejoiced that at last he was having a care for others. With tears in their eyes, they gave him their blessing and watched him ride off in his new, shining armour and spotless white surcoat, with the lad following proudly, now promoted to the rank of page.

For some time life continued peacefully on Wearside, and the worm remained in the well, growing daily, until eventually it filled the whole well and it realized that it would have to climb out and find a new home.

Carefully, it explored the swiftly flowing River Wear and its green banks crowned with magnificent trees, and finally it decided that, by day, it would live on a large rock in the middle of the river, and in the evening, it would make its way to an oval hill on the north bank of the Wear, about a mile and a half from Lambton Hall. When it first went there, it could just coil round the base of the hill so that its nose was within a few inches of the tip of its scaly tail, but so fast did it continue growing that before very long it could wind itself three times round the hill.

All this growing meant that the worm had an appetite which increased daily, so that the time came when it was no longer content with catching and devouring whole raw fish and eels, and it began to turn its attention to the nearby cottages and farms.

Early in the morning, before the milkmaids were stirring, it would suck the cows' milk so that not a drop was left for the household; no egg in a nest was ever safe, no matter how high the parent birds had built their home, nor how cunningly they had hidden it in the river bank. Ducks and chickens, rabbits and moorhens disappeared at an alarming rate, and any young piglet which strayed from its mother's side or any lamb which frisked too far afield was immediately snapped up by the worm.

Each day it sharpened its terrible claws and pointed teeth on the trunks of the trees, tearing them up by the roots and leaving them, torn and mangled, on the grass which was burnt brown by its fiery breath, and so it was not long before it had laid waste the whole of the north bank of the Wear. All the farms and cottages were deserted, because those who had lived in them, terrified that any day the worm might start to eat them, had fled to friends and relations as far from the dreadful creature as possible.

When the worm had brought utter ruin and desolation to the north bank, it turned its attention to the south. Crossing the swift-flowing river, it dealt summarily with a foolish hare, an inquisitive owl and a couple of bats, and, lying down, it contemplated Lambton Hall thoughtfully, fire gushing from its nostrils, and its scaly tail swinging idly backwards and forwards, backwards and forwards.

When the servants saw the creature on their side of the river bank, they ran about panic-stricken, locking and bolting all the doors, closing the shutters over the windows and wringing their hands in anguish, until at length the old lord called everyone into the hall to discuss what they ought to do about the terrible worm outside.

There was any amount of weeping and wailing from the women servants, who had no wish to end up as a tasty meal for the worm – although secretly the old lord couldn't help thinking that most of them would prove much too tough even for the worm. And there was any amount of talking and arguing from the men servants, who all thought that some-one should go out and kill the creature at once – as long as it wasn't them.

'You can't kill it,' the steward said flatly. 'I know for a fact that two of the strongest woodcutters from up the dale tried, only last week, to kill it with their axes. For hours they fought on the bank, and finally one cut off a leg, while the other sliced clean through the creature's tail and sent it flying. But this is no ordinary worm. Do you know what hap-pened? The leg simply joined itself on again, and the tail jumped back into place.'

'Woodcutters with axes are no use against the worm,' the old lord said. 'We must send to the Lord Bishop of Durham, and ask him to lend us some of his knights to deal with the creature.'

'And in the meantime?' the steward asked.

'What do you mean, steward?'

'It will take at least a week for our messenger to reach Durham, and for the Lord Bishop to summon his knights

and send them here. By that time the worm will probably
have had most of us for breakfast – the young ones, at any
rate.'

At this the kitchen-maid screamed, threw her pinafore over
her face and collapsed in hysterics. She was quite definitely
the youngest person in Lambton Hall, and the boot-boy had
just plucked up his courage and asked her to go to the next
fair at Durham with him, and how could she do that if she
was inside the terrible worm?

'What do you suggest, steward?' the old lord asked.

As the steward had no suggestions to make, the lady, realizing that the menfolk were getting nowhere, took charge of
things.

'In the courtyard there is a large trough from which the
horses drink,' she said. 'I want you men to get all the pails
and buckets you can find, and empty out the water, and then
I want you women to carry the milk from the dairy and pour
it into the trough, and after that we must wait and see what
happens.'

Hurriedly they all did as they were told, running back to
the Hall the moment the trough was filled with milk, bolting
the door and then peering anxiously out of the upstairs
windows – all except the kitchen-maid, who was being com-
forted in the pantry by the boot-boy.

Curiously the worm approached, dragging its long length
over the grass and across the courtyard. Bending over the
trough it peered short-sightedly at the contents. The white
liquid looked like milk. The worm sniffed. It smelled like
milk. Cautiously a forked tongue darted out and in. Yes it
was milk!

Without more ado, the worm settled down and never lifted
its head until it had licked the trough dry. Hiccupping loudly,
it looked up at the faces peering out at it from the Hall
windows, nodded its head to show that it was satisfied for
the time being and then, making its way back to its favourite
hill, wound itself three times round the base and fell fast
asleep.

The next day, one of the servants posted on the roof dashed down to say that the worm was crossing the river and making for the Hall again. Hastily all the milk in the dairy was emptied into the trough, and again the worm drank, nodded, and departed satisfied.

But it took the milk of nine cows to fill that trough, and inevitably the day came, before the Lord Bishop's knights arrived, when the lady of the Hall had only enough milk to half-fill the trough.

When the worm saw this, its rage was terrible. Advancing on the trees in the park it lashed out at them with its powerful tail, while at the same time it seized others between its jaws and tore them up by their roots, so that when at last it departed, so fearful was the destruction and devastation, that the lady burst into tears and it was a long time before the lord could comfort her.

Things were no better when at last the Lord Bishop sent his trained knights, for even though they knew how to thrust and parry, how to defend themselves and probe the weakness of the enemy, they found themselves completely powerless in dealing with this creature whose limbs jumped back into place as soon as they were cut off.

'If only our son had been here, he would have slain the worm,' the old lord mourned. But their son was in the Holy Land, and knew nothing of the terrible creature which he had caught that Sunday morning, and had thrown so carelessly into the well.

In desperation, the people of Weardale took it in turns to send their milk up to Lambton Hall, so that the trough might be filled every day: but if ever there was not enough, or if the carriers were late, then the worm raged and stormed, destroying everything in its path so that nothing grew on either bank of the Wear – neither grass, nor crops, nor trees.

So seven long years passed.

The old lord and his wife were tired and heart-broken, knowing that they could not live much longer under the tyranny of the dreadful worm, while such people as still stayed in Weardale looked pale and worn, jumping at the slightest sound, afraid that any hour might be their last, for the worm had taken to eating men and women if the trough was not full to the brim with fresh milk.

On the last day of the seventh year, the heir of Lambton returned from the Crusades a knight. His armour was holed and dinted, his surcoat stained and torn, and his face brown and scarred, while no one recognized his page, so tall and broad had he grown. When the heir saw the state of the countryside and heard of the terror spread by the worm which he himself had caught seven years ago, on a Sunday morning, and had tossed so carelessly into the well, he was horrified and ashamed. During the years he had been away, he had learned, among a great many other things, that it was a knight's duty to care for others who were not capable of looking after themselves.

Well he knew that he was responsible for the presence of the terrible worm, and he was all for setting out there and then to slay the creature – until he heard of its power to join its severed limbs.

'I have the strength to fight the worm,' he said to his parents, 'but what is needed is cunning. Does the Wise Woman still live in the cottage by the three elm trees?'

'She does,' his mother answered.

'I shall go to ask for her advice tonight,' the heir said.

'Take with you the last dove from the dovecot, the last jar of plover's eggs in aspic, and the last flagon of ale,' his mother said. 'Don't give them to her, as she never accepts payment for her advice, but leave them on the convenient shelf at her back door. Rest assured that she will see what you have brought before she hears why you have come.'

That evening the heir presented himself at the back door of the cottage by the three elm trees, placed on the convenient shelf the gifts which his mother had suggested, and knocked boldly on the door.

'Who is that who knocks so boldly on my door?' a voice cried.

'The heir of Lambton, returned from the Holy Land, seeking advice as to how he can destroy the worm.'

'Go round to the front door, heir of Lambton,' the voice
ordered, and as the heir walked round, he heard the back
door being unbolted.

The Wise Woman was obviously very pleased with her
gifts, because when she opened the front door and bade the
heir enter, she contented herself with upbraiding him for a
mere half-hour for having brought the terrible worm to
Weardale, and then she allowed him to apologize and explain
that he was indeed a very changed man from the thoughtless
youth of seven years previously. All that he wanted, he
assured her, was that she, who was wiser than anyone else in
the whole of the North of England, should help him to get
rid of the terrible worm.

'It can be done,' she answered. 'Now listen closely. Stud
your armour with sharp spear heads, so that anything which
comes in contact with it will be cut immediately. Then, with
your good sword in your right hand, go down to the swift
flowing river and take your stand on the rock in the middle,
just before the setting of the sun, and attack the worm
when it returns from its hill, and while it is still standing
in the Wear.'

'How can I ever thank you enough?' the heir asked, springing to his feet to go.

'Don't be in such a hurry, young man. There is yet more
to be done. Before you go back to your home, you must take
a vow in the church by the river, promising that if you are
successful and slay the worm, you will kill the first living
thing that you meet on your way back to the Hall. If you fail
to keep this vow, then I warn you that for nine generations
no lord of Lambton will die in his bed.'

Pondering over all that the Wise Woman had said, the heir
made his way down to the little church by the river, and there
he vowed that if he was successful and slew the worm, he
would kill the first living thing that he met on his way back
to the Hall.

All the next day, as he and his page studded his armour with sharp spear heads, he thought about the vow, until at last he knew exactly what he must do.

Late the following day he put on his spear-studded armour, slung his bugle over his shoulder, and taking his good sword in his right hand, turned to his parents, who were watching him anxiously, afraid that they might never see him again, so terrible was the worm.

'Have no fear for me,' he said, 'but listen carefully to what I have to say. When I leave here to go down to the river, lock and bolt all the doors. When the fight is over, and if I am the victor, as I hope to be, I shall blow three notes on my bugle. Then, Father, open the door so that my page can release one of the hounds, to be the first living thing to meet me on my way back here.'

'I will do as you say,' the old lord promised, and the heir left the Hall, walked down to the river, and took his stand on the rock in the middle just before the setting of the sun.

A few minutes later the worm uncoiled itself from its hill and made its way back to the Wear, hissing fiercely as it saw the heir standing on its rock. Plunging into the river, it lashed out with its powerful tail, catching the heir round the waist, and then coil upon coil wound itself round him, to crush him to death, as the worm had crushed many another knight.

But the creature had reckoned without the spear heads. The tighter the coils closed on the heir the worse the wounds it inflicted on itself, each spear head cutting deeper and deeper into its scaly skin. Weaker and weaker grew the worm from loss of blood, until at last the heir was able to free his sword arm, and with a single stroke, cut off the creature's head. Immediately the swift-flowing river carried off the head before it had time to join itself to the neck again.

And that was the end of the terrible Lambton worm.

Joyfully the heir raised his bugle – now rather squashed – to his lips and blew three long, loud notes.

'My son has slain the worm,' the old lord cried, and for-

getting everything except the fact that his son was alive, he unbolted the door and ran down to the river to greet his son.

When the heir saw his father, he was horrified. He had made a vow, but he could not possibly kill his own father. Anguished, he lifted his horn to his lips a second time, and again he blew three long, loud notes.

This time his page released one of the hounds, which reached the heir first and so he was able to keep his vow and kill it.

The Wise Woman, however, was not to be tricked in such a manner. That evening, when everyone in Weardale was feasting in Lambton Hall, and rejoicing that the heir had slain the terrible worm, she descended on them wrathfully.

'You broke your vow,' she thundered. 'Now my curse shall lie on this house, and for nine generations no lord of Lambton will die in his bed.'

'Surely you didn't expect my son to kill his own father?' the lady of the Hall pleaded.

'He should have thought of that before he made the vow,' the Wise Woman answered stiffly, and then, looking at the downcast faces round the table, she threw back her head and laughed.

'Use your wits,' she cried, bending down and prodding the heir with a bony elbow. 'Is it really such a terrible thing not to die in your bed? If you could choose, would you die miserably at home or gloriously in battle?'

'Gloriously in battle, of course,' the heir answered, and everyone smiled, suddenly realizing that the Wise Woman's condition was not a curse, but a blessing.

And so it was that nine generations of Lambtons died bravely and honourably in battle, and should you ever be in County Durham, in the North of England, you can see for yourself the new Lambton Castle which was built on the site of the old hall, and the Worm Hill, around which the worm coiled its scaly length for seven long, dreadful years.

7

THE BLACK BULL OF NORROWAY

Once upon a time there lived in Norroway a widow with three daughters. The eldest was good-looking and vain: the second good-looking and foolish: but as for the youngest, she worked so hard looking after her mother and sisters, cultivating the ground beside the cottage and caring for the pig and hens that she had neither the time nor the wish to find out what she looked like.

One day the eldest daughter said to her mother, 'Bake me a bannock and roast me a collop, Mother. It is time I left here and found myself a rich husband who will give me a golden carriage drawn by six white horses.'

The widow baked a thick oatmeal scone, cooked a pork chop, and the eldest daughter set off. All day she walked until at last she came to a hovel where there lived a witch-washerwoman and her ugly daughter, and there she told them what she wanted.

'Look out of my back door,' the witch-washerwoman ordered, and though the eldest daughter stared out the whole of the next day, and the next, she saw nothing except the washing spread out on the bushes to dry. On the third day, however, she saw a golden coach drawn by six white horses. 'Yon's what you want,' the witch cried, and the eldest daughter leaped inside and drove off, and for all anyone knows she lived as happily as could be expected.

Before very long the second daughter said, 'Bake me a bannock and roast me a collop, Mother. It is time I left here and found myself a rich husband who will give me a carriage of silver drawn by four chestnut horses.'

The widow baked a thick oatmeal scone, cooked a pork chop, and the second daughter set off. All day she walked, until at last she came to the hovel where the witch-washerwoman and her ugly daughter lived, and there she told them what she wanted.

'Look out of my back door,' the witch ordered, and though the second daughter stared out the whole of the next day, and the next, she saw nothing except the washing spread out on the grass to dry. On the third day, however, she saw a silver coach drawn by four chestnut horses. 'Yon's what you want,' the witch cried, and the second daughter leaped inside and drove off, and for all anyone knows she lived as happily as she deserved.

At last the time came when it was the turn of the youngest daughter. 'Bake me a bannock and roast me a collop, Mother,' she said. 'It is time that I left here and found a husband to love, and when that happens, I shall send for you to come and live with us so that you will have no more cares in the world.'

For the third time the widow baked and cooked, and the youngest daughter set off, walking until she came to the witch's hovel.

'If all you want is a husband to love, look out of my back door,' the witch cried, and though the girl stared out the whole of the next day, and the next, she saw nothing except the witch and her ugly daughter pounding the washing with flat stones down beside the stream. On the third day, however, she saw a huge Black Bull come roaring down the road. 'Yon's what you want,' the witch said, and tossed the girl up on to the back of the Bull, and off the beast went, without so much as a glance at her, galloping through woods and meadows and over hedges and streams, until at length the girl felt weak with hunger.

'Eat out of my right ear and drink out of my left,' the Bull said, although she had not spoken a word, 'and scatter what's left for the birds and wild creatures.'

The girl ate from the loaf in the Bull's right ear, and drank from the flask in its left, threw away what was left for the birds and wild creatures, and on they rode again.

Just as the sun was setting they came to a big, grey castle.

'Yon belongs to my eldest brother,' the Bull said, 'and we shall spend the night there.' The girl was welcomed, feasted and given a splendid bedroom in which to sleep, while the Bull was taken away through the park to a lush, green field.

After breakfast the next morning, the girl was given a beautiful wine-red glass apple, and was told that only if she was in great danger was she to break it. As she was helped on to the back of the Bull, the creature glanced at her for a moment with sad, brown eyes, and then they were off at a gallop through woods and meadows and over hedges and streams.

When the girl was weak with hunger, the Bull bade her do as she had done on the previous day, and she ate from his right ear and drank from his left and scattered what was left for the birds and wild creatures. On they rode again, and just as the sun was setting they came to a castle that was twice as big as the previous one.

'Yon belongs to my second brother,' the Bull said, 'and we shall spend the night there.' The girl was welcomed, feasted and given a splendid bedroom in which to sleep, while the Bull was taken away through the park to a lush, green field.

After breakfast the next morning, the girl was given a beautiful saffron-yellow glass pear, and was told that only if she was in greater danger than she had ever thought possible was she to break it.

As she was helped on to the back of the Bull, his eyes lingered on her, as though there was something he desperately wanted to say and either could not or dare not speak, and then they were off at a gallop, through woods and meadows and over hedges and streams.

When the girl was weak with hunger, she ate from the Bull's right ear and drank from his left and scattered what was left for the birds and wild creatures. On they rode again, and just as the sun was setting they came to the biggest and most magnificent castle the girl had ever seen.

'Yon belongs to my third brother,' the Bull said, 'and we shall spend the night there.' The girl was welcomed, feasted, and given a splendid bedroom in which to sleep, while the Bull was taken away through the park to a lush, green field.

After breakfast the next morning, the girl was given a beautiful russet-brown glass plum, and told that only if she was in danger of losing what she held most dear was she to break it.

Again the Bull looked at her beseechingly as the girl was helped on to his back, but this time when he set off he walked slowly, as though he wanted to save his strength and energy. At length they came to a dark valley where withered and leafless trees huddled together; huge stinging nettles grew through trailing, thorned briars and giant hemlock grew side by side with deadly nightshade; in the sky above there was no singing of little birds, nor in the rank undergrowth was there the scampering of wild creatures.

'Now we have come to the end of my journey,' the Bull said, 'and the place where I must fight my enemy, the Old Enchanter. Go and sit on yon fallen tree trunk, and do not move so much as one single muscle or I shall never be able to find you again. Just sit and wait as though you had been carved from stone. If the valley turns blue, I shall have conquered the Old Enchanter, but if it turns red, then he will have defeated me.'

The girl slipped down from the back of the Bull and sat on the fallen tree trunk, as still as though she had been carved from stone, until suddenly the whole valley turned blue – and in the far distance she saw the Bull. But even as she recognized him he faded, and in his place stood a wounded knight, his armour dented, his clothes stained with blood.

Forgetting what she had been told, the girl leaned forward a fraction of an inch, the better to see, whereupon the knight vanished as the Bull had done, and the blue light faded, and there was nothing left but the dark valley with its nettles and briar, its hemlock and nightshade – and when the Bull returned for her, he could not find her.

All evening the girl sat, and all through the night, crying and calling to the Bull that she was waiting for him on the

fallen tree trunk, but at last, when the sun rose above the huddled trees, she gave up all hope, stumbled to her feet and walked wearily away, not knowing where she was or whither she was going.

On she walked until she came to a great glass mountain, and as it was obvious that there was no way over it, she began to walk round it. Just as her strength was giving out, she came to the forge of a blacksmith, and so dirty and dishevelled was she that at first he thought she was a lad looking for work, and as he needed an apprentice, he offered to take her on there and then.

When he heard her story, he stood by his offer. 'Serve a seven years' apprenticeship with me,' he said, 'and at the end of the time I'll make you iron shoes with spikes in the soles so that you can climb the glass mountain.'

Gratefully the girl accepted the offer, and at the end of the seven years the smith begged her to stay on as she was the best apprentice he'd ever had, and could shoe a horse better than many a man. Realizing, however, that the girl's heart was set on finding the Black Bull, he kept his promise and made her iron shoes with spikes in the soles.

With the help of the shoes she climbed the glass mountain, and then she threw them away; barefoot, she journeyed on day after day, living off nuts and wild fruits and crusts thrown to her as she passed through poor hamlets, until at last she came to the cottage where the witch-washerwoman and her ugly daughter dwelt.

'Your sisters never came back, so they were easily satisfied,' the witch said, as she bent over the stream and pounded with a stone at blood-stained garments. 'What is it that you want now?'

'What I have always wanted – a husband to love,' the girl said wearily. 'Give me something to eat and I will work for you until I am strong enough to continue my search.'

'The knight from yon castle has announced that he will marry the girl who can wash these stains from his battle garments. Many girls have tried, including my own daughter, but you can see for yourself that not all the rubbing or scrubbing or wringing has the slightest effect. Roll up your sleeves and see what you can do.'

The girl rolled up her sleeves, dipped the garments in the stream, and when she had wrung them out, all the stains had disappeared.

At first the witch did not know whether to be pleased or angry, but presently she formed her plan. She brought more washing down to the stream to keep the girl busy all day, and then she returned to her cottage and dragged out a chest full of costly dresses and jewellery. After the ugly daughter had washed her face and hair, the witch dressed her up in the splendid garments so that she looked almost like a lady, and then the two of them set off for the castle with the knight's battle garments.

When the knight saw the garments with the blood-stains of battle removed, he sent for all his people and announced that he would marry the witch's daughter that very day, and and gave orders that rooms should be prepared for mother and daughter in the castle.

Everyone rejoiced and cheered loudly – all except the girl, who stood at the back of the hall and now knew that here was the knight who had been bewitched by the Old Enchanter and turned into a Black Bull, and she knew that although she loved him dearly, he could not see her because she had disobeyed him and leaned forward a fraction of an inch in the dark valley.

Realizing that she was in great danger from the witch and her daughter, she broke open her beautiful wine-red glass apple and found it crammed full of glittering, shining golden coins.

At once she sought out the witch's daughter, and offered her the coins if she would put off her wedding for one day, and allow her to sit on a chair by the open window of the knight's bedroom. Greedily the witch's daughter took the coins, but when she told her mother what she had agreed, the witch prepared a sleeping draught and gave it to the knight just before he went to bed, so that he fell asleep immediately and never once stirred.

All night long the knight slept his drugged sleep, while on a chair by the open window the girl sat, alternately weeping and singing –

> Seven long years I served for thee,
> The glassy hill I clomb for thee,
> Thy bloody clothes I wrang for thee;
> And wilt thou not waken and turn to me?

But the knight heard nothing, and just before dawn the witch came in and led the girl away, before the effects of the potion wore off.

Realizing that she was now in greater danger from the witch and her daughter than she had ever thought possible, the girl broke open her beautiful saffron-yellow glass pear and found it full of precious stones – emeralds, topazes, pearls and diamonds – and all these she offered the witch's daughter if she would put off her wedding for yet another day and allow her to sit on a chair by the open window of the knight's bedroom.

Greedily the witch's daughter took the precious stones, but when her mother heard about it, she gave the knight another sleeping draught, so that all night long he slept his drugged sleep, while the girl sat by the window, alternately weeping and singing –

> Seven long years I served for thee,
> The glassy hill I clomb for thee,
> Thy bloody clothes I wrang for thee;
> And wilt thou not waken and turn to me?

But the knight heard nothing, and just before dawn the witch came in and led the weeping girl away, before the effects of the potion wore off.

Realizing that now she was in danger of losing what she held most dear – a husband to love – the girl broke open her beautiful russet-brown glass plum, and found there the most exquisite jewellery, delicately fashioned by a master craftsman from the finest gold and silver and the choicest of precious stones, and all these she gave to the witch's daughter to postpone the wedding for but one more day.

That morning, when the knight was out hunting, one of his friends asked him who it was that had been alternately weeping and singing at his bedroom window the two previous nights. The knight answered that he had heard nothing, but when others insisted that they too had heard the song, and even repeated fragments of it to him, he fell silent, and not a word did he speak to anyone for the rest of the day. That evening, however, when the witch brought him his sleeping draught, he despatched her on some errand and in her absence threw the potion out of the window, but gave every appearance of being sound asleep when the witch returned.

Still and silent he lay in his bed as the witch departed: still and silent he lay as the girl came in, paused by his bed and sighed heavily, and then taking her seat by the window, began to sing –

> Seven long years I served for thee,
> The glassy hill I clomb for thee,
> Thy bloody clothes I wrang for thee;
> And wilt thou not waken and turn to me?

At last the knight heard, and turned to her and recognized the girl he had fallen in love with while he was under the curse of the Old Enchanter. He told her all that had happened since he lost her when she leaned forward the better to see him in the dark valley, and she told him all that had happened to her in her search to find him again.

The wedding took place that day, but it was the faithful girl he married and not the witch's daughter – she and her mother he banished from his lands. Then he sent for the girl's mother and gave her rooms and attendants of her own and they all lived happily ever after in the far-off land of Norroway.

8

THE BLACK LAD MacCRIMMON

Long ago there lived on the misty island of Skye a family by the name of MacCrimmon. The father was a big, burly man, who could give a fine account of himself in battle if need be, but his first love was not for fighting but for music.

It was splendid to see and even more splendid to hear when he took up his bagpipes – which he called the Black Gate – and putting the reed of the pipe or chanter between his lips and his fingers on the stops, he would walk slowly up and down outside the castle of Dunvegan, home of the MacLeod of MacLeod, and filled the air with wild, martial music.

'No one on the island of Skye can play the bagpipes like MacCrimmon, piper to the MacLeod of MacLeod,' men said, when first they heard him play; but when he had finished playing, they sighed and shook their heads.

'No one in the whole of Scotland can play the bagpipes like MacCrimmon,' they said, and the wild music remained ringing in their ears, haunting them for days after, and all the other chieftains who lived on the Islands of the Hebrides, and on the mainland of Scotland, envied the MacLeod of MacLeod his splendid piper.

Now MacCrimmon – whose wife had died long before – had three sons.

The first two were fine, burly fellows like their father, with his gift for playing the bagpipes and sending men's blood throbbing through their veins, and the father had high hopes that, when they were as old and experienced as he was, they would be almost as great. No one, he declared flatly, would ever be the master of the pipes that he himself was. And of course his two sons – and everyone else who'd ever heard him play – agreed.

The third son was a bitter disappointment.

To begin with, he wasn't particularly tall, nor was he particularly strong: he cared little for fighting, but what was worst of all in the eyes of his father and brothers – he could not play the bagpipes.

It was not for want of trying on his part or beating on his father's. The lad just hadn't a note of music in him. Practise as he might, all he ever succeeded in producing was a wailing and moaning which nearly drove his father mad so that finally he would snatch the pipes from his youngest son, cuff him roundly and send him off to clean the cottage or cook the meal; he'd have sent him to card and spin too, if he hadn't broken his wife's spinning wheel in a fit of temper.

'Woman's work – that's all you're fit for,' he exclaimed, as again and again the lad failed to coax out the music which lay in the bagpipes.

'Woman's work,' his two elder brothers agreed, leaving him to light the peat fire, make porridge in the iron pot which hung above it, and then take out the flat girdle and bake oatcakes for their breakfast.

Now the day came when there was a great fair on the mainland, and his father with the Black Gate, and his two brothers with their bagpipes, pulled their boat down from the shingle where it was beached and prepared to row across from the island, to play to the crowds who would have gathered from afar and to bring yet more renown to the name of MacCrimmon and their chieftain the MacLeod of MacLeod.

'May I come with you to the fair?' the youngest son asked.

'Not until you can play the bagpipes, and be a credit to the name of MacCrimmon,' his father answered brusquely.

'And that will be never,' his eldest brother said.

'All he's fit for is woman's work,' the second added, and laughing scornfully, they rowed across the sea to the fair on the mainland.

It's not for want of trying on my part, and beating on my father's, that I cannot master the pipes, the lad thought sadly. Taking down his chanter – the pipe with the finger holes, on which the melody is played – he wandered out of doors, making for the hills whose heads were lost in the swirling mist, because he had found that, no matter how unhappy he was, if he could only walk and climb among the lonely hills until he was utterly exhausted, he could always find a strange and comforting peace.

He had not gone very far when he met coming from the moors a very old woman, bent almost double under a load of peat. Not of course that there was anything unusual about this. Much of the hard physical work on the crofts and the carrying of heavy burdens, as well as the housework and spinning and weaving, was done by the women of the Hebrides in those days; but the lad had a tender heart, and the woman was so old that she looked as though she might collapse under her load at any moment.

'Good day to you, Old Woman,' he said. 'Have you no daughter or grand-daughter to carry that load of peat for you?'

'I have no one at all,' the old woman snapped. 'And it would be too much for a weakling like you should ever it enter your head to offer to carry it.'

'If I am a weakling, it is not my fault, nor the fault of my father,' the lad said. 'But I am accustomed to woman's work and so I shall carry the peat for you.'

Without a word of thanks the old woman relinquished her sack and strode on ahead, leaving the lad to pick it up and follow her.

For an old woman, she is remarkably spry, he thought, struggling to keep up with her as they climbed higher and higher into the hills.

For an old woman she is remarkably strong, he thought, as the load appeared to grow heavier and heavier on his back so that he feared that never again would he be able to stand upright. Looking down, he envied the wild white swans resting on the still waters of a lochan far below, and looking up he envied the golden eagle brooding in its eyrie in the cleft near the top of the crags.

Higher and higher they climbed until the mists came down suddenly and shrouded the island below and the hill tops above, and just when the lad was about to call out that he could not climb another foot, the old woman stopped in front of a wall of grey rock, stamped her foot three times, and watched as a door swung noiselessly open.

Now the lad knew what indeed he had suspected for some time, that this was no ordinary woman, but the Fairy Woman of the Cave of Gold. He was more frightened than he had ever been before because you never knew where you were with fairies: if they liked you, they might help you or do you a favour; they had even been known to make a man's fortune for him; but if they took a dislike to you, they could cause some very odd and peculiar things to happen.

'Why on earth are you carrying that sack of stones all the way up into the hills when there are stones enough here?' the Fairy Woman asked scornfully.

'Stones?' Wearily the lad swung the sack down and stared at its contents. It had been full of peat when he'd picked it up, but now it was full of sharp, heavy stones, and he knew that his shoulders and back must be bruised and bleeding.

'As you've given yourself the trouble of climbing up here after me, the least you can do is entertain me,' the Fairy Woman snapped, entering the mouth of the cave and sitting down with a sigh, as though she were the one who was weary from carrying the heavy sack. 'Take the chanter out of your pocket and come inside and play me something.'

The lad groaned. If the Fairy Woman were in a bad temper now, what would she be like when she heard the miserable noises which were all he could produce? If she didn't strike him dead on the spot – which, all things considered, might be a merciful release – she'd probably turn him into a hare and set the dogs on to him, or change him into a herring in the sea and send a giant gannet hurtling down from the sky to put an end to his miserable existence.

'Alas!' he said mournfully. 'I can no more play the chanter which is in my pocket than I can fly, though it is not for the want of trying on my part, or of beating on my father's.'

'Step over to the shelf on the far side of the cave and bring me the silver chanter which you will find there.'

Resigned now to whatever the fates and the fairies might have in store for him, the lad stepped over to the shelf and brought back the silver chanter which he found there.

'Now play it,' the Fairy Woman commanded.

For a little while she listened to the wailing discordance which the lad produced, and then she signed to him to stop.

'If murdering music were a crime, you would have been hanged from the nearest tree many a long year past,' she commented. 'Now let us see if you lack sense as you so obviously lack the gift of music. Answer me this. Which would you choose, skill without success, or success without skill?'

'Long and painful are the hours I have spent in a fruitless endeavour to acquire skill and please my father and brothers, so the skill must fend for itself and I'd choose success.'

'Very well.'

Pulling a long grey hair from her head, the Fairy Woman gave it to the lad, bidding him twist it round the reed of the silver chanter, and as he did so it changed from grey to gold. When he looked up in surprise it was to find that the Fairy Woman's hair was now a beautiful gold, although her face was still old and wrinkled.

'No lass on the island has hair as beautiful as yours,' he said; but if she was pleased, she showed no sign of it.

'Put your fingers on the holes of the chanter,' she ordered, and when he had done so, she came round behind him and, reaching over, she placed her wrinkled fingers on top of his young ones. 'When I raise one finger, then you lift the finger which is underneath: when I raise another, you raise yours. Now, think of some tune which you wish to play and do what I have told you.'

The lad thought of a lament which had been in his head for some time, and which no one had ever played before, and watching the fingers on top of his, he raised his own in turn, and the Cave of Gold was filled with the saddest, sweetest music it had ever known.

When at last the tune was finished and the sobbing music had died away, the lad turned round to thank the Fairy Woman, only to find that the years had fled from her face and stooping body, and it was a young and beautiful creature who watched him with a smile of approval.

'Now you are the King of Pipers, lad. Your equal was not before you, and your equal shall not be after you.'

The next moment a gust of wind blew the swirling mists into the cave, setting the lad coughing and choking, and by the time he had groped his way to the entrance, the mist suddenly lifted, and when he turned round, both the Fairy Woman and the entrance to the Cave of Gold had completely disappeared.

I must have imagined it all, the lad thought, lifting to his mouth the silver chanter with the golden thread still wound round its reed. Immediately the air trembled to the magic of his music, and the golden eagle in its eyrie above and the wild swans on the lochan below stretched their necks and closed their eyes as the music played about them.

Down the hill track walked the lad, playing all the time the tunes which his father and brothers, his grandfather and great-grandfather had played, and his father and brothers, rowing back over the sea, heard him and exchanged glances, but said never a word.

That evening, after the lad had prepared the meal and they had all eaten, the father lifted up his own pipes, the Black Gate, and marching up and down on the grassy headland above the shores of Loch Dunvegan, he played a stirring air in praise of the MacLeod of MacLeod, whose seat was at Dunvegan Castle.

After him, the eldest son took up his pipes and played a mournful lament for the heroes who had fallen in battle and were mourned by their wives and children.

Last of all the second son played – this time a gay dance for the times of peace, when food and drink were plentiful, and a man could express the joy in his heart through the nimbleness of his feet.

When he had finished, the father took his own Black Gate and handed them to the lad.

'Here you are,' he said. 'Play.'

The lad was astounded.

'I am not worthy of such an honour,' he stammered. 'All I am fit for is woman's work.'

But he took the Black Gate from his father and, if he had played well before when he left the Fairy Woman of the Cave of Gold, he played a thousand times better now, for the airs he played were of his own composition, compounded of his dreams, of the beauty of the misty island of Skye which had been for centuries the home of the MacCrimmons, and of the pride and valour of his chieftain, the MacLeod of MacLeod.

When at last he came to an end of playing and would have handed back the Black Gate, his father shook his head.

'The Black Gate is yours, and from today men shall know you as the Black Lad MacCrimmon. And this I tell you – none of us will ever come in your wake, for the music has left us.'

The Black Lad knew then that the Fairy Woman had indeed spoken the truth, and that his equal had never been before him, and his equal should not be after him.

Although his sons and grandsons and great-grandsons lacked in their playing that special magic which the Fairy Woman had bestowed on the Black Lad, yet, with the help of the silver chanter and the golden thread wound round its reed, for generations the MacCrimmons were the most famous of Scottish pipers, and men came from near and far to learn from them on their island home.

So if, by any chance, you ever sail over the sea to Skye, then climb the headland which overlooks the western shores of Loch Dunvegan, and at the clachan of Boreraig you will find a great stone cairn, erected to the memory of the Mac-Crimmons, for centuries pipers to the MacLeod of MacLeod.

But what happened to the silver chanter and the golden hair wound round its reed, and whether the Black Lad owed his gifts to his own skill and perseverance after all – these are questions which no one can answer now.

9

THE SKIPPER, THE LAD AND THE PEOPLE OF PEACE

Long, long ago, in the green morning of time, there dwelt on the northern coast of Scotland a poor lad who had neither kith nor kin. He lived in a turf hut of his own building and he made enough to keep body and soul together by working from time to time for the fishermen and crofters who lived nearby round the rocky bay.

In return for his labours at sea or on land, he was paid in cast-off clothing, potatoes, oatmeal, herring and goatsmilk: some would have given more if they had had it, but a fisherman's life was a hazardous one and its rewards were poor, and a man was hard put to it to look after his own family without bothering about a lad who had no claim on him.

Now at the opposite end of the bay an old skipper lived in conditions which were not much better than those of the lad. In his day he had been the captain of a fishing boat, and many a fine catch he and his crew had landed when the sea was in a generous mood and herring shoals sighted off the coast.

But the sea is a dangerous master, even for those who know how to scan the skies for a coming storm, watch the flighting of the birds for some unsuspected danger: one by one it claimed the members of his crew until finally it rose in wrath and plunged on his ship, driving it on to the jagged rocks where it foundered and sank.

As the skipper had no money to buy a new boat, and was too old to crew for younger men, he was reduced to fishing from the shore or hunting the rock pools for the occasional crab or lobster, and for shrimps, mussels and cockles which he took home and boiled and ate with oatcakes of his own baking.

Now it happened that one day as he was searching the
high-water mark for driftwood and dried seaweed with which
to feed his fire, he looked up to find a little man beside
him, staring at him curiously. Surprised – because he had
not heard the little man approach – he returned the stare,
noticing that he was wearing a leather jerkin of the kind
that had not been worn since his great-grandfather's day,
and a red cap whose like he had never seen before.

'They tell me that in your day you were captain of your
own boat,' the little man said, 'and that you still know the
tides and races, the islands and submerged rocks better than
any man on the north coast of Scotland.'

'They tell you true,' the skipper answered.

'How would you like to have charge of a vessel again?'
the little man asked.

'I am grown too old,' the skipper said sadly. 'My arms have
lost their strength and my eyes are no longer keen enough
for anyone to trust me with his boat.'

'I have a boat but it lacks a skipper; come down to the
shore and tell me if you are prepared to sail it for me and
mine.'

Scarcely able to believe his ears, the skipper followed the
little man down to the shore, but his heart sank when he
saw the pitiful wreck beached there, with its rotting planks
and gaping seams, its mast which lacked sails and its useless
rudder.

'No man in his senses would put to sea in a wreck like that,'
he cried.

'It is true that it lacks this and that,' the little man agreed,
'but if you will hire a sailor to crew for you and come
back in three days, I assure you that the vessel will be
ready.'

I suppose he knows what he's talking about, the skipper
thought, and he made for the cluster of cottages where the
fishermen and crofters lived.

'I have come to seek a man to crew for me in three days'
time,' he said.

'Crew for you?' they repeated. 'Where is your vessel, old skipper?'

'Down on the shore.'

Filled with curiosity they all stopped whatever they were doing, and the men and their wives and children hurried down to the shore.

When they saw the pitiful wreck with its rotting planks and gaping seams, its mast which lacked sails and its useless rudder, they burst out into raucous laughter, digging one another in the ribs, holding their aching sides and bending nearly double with mirth at the idea of anyone even contemplating putting to sea in such a wretched vessel.

'You'll have to whistle for a crew as well as for a wind,' they cried mockingly, and, still laughing, they went back to tend their crops while their wives prepared the lines for the night's fishing.

Only the poor lad remained behind on the shore with the skipper: there had been no work for him for several days, and having just eaten the last of his porridge, he was wondering where the next meal was coming from.

'If you will have me, I will crew for you,' he said.

'I will have you. Come back in three days and the vessel will be ready to sail,' the skipper said; and they both returned to their homes, wondering how this could possibly be so.

The lad went off to the moors above the bay, caught a rabbit and made himself a fine stew, while the skipper baked the last of his oatmeal and lost himself in dreams of the days when he had been young and strong and his vessel had been the best manned and maintained along the whole of the coast.

On the third day the skipper and the lad went down to the beach where the vessel was now lying at anchor. True, there had been some attempt to replace some of the rotting planks, to fill the gaping seams, but in place of the sails which were vital when the captain carried only a crew of one, the mast was hung with tattered old rags.

'They're crazy, the skipper and the lad,' the other fishermen cried, coming down to the shore and seeing the state the vessel was in. 'The boat'll founder and they'll both be drowned before they're even out of sight of land.' They began to argue with the skipper, pointing out how unseaworthy the entire vessel was, and when he refused to listen to them, they would have restrained him forcibly from boarding her – except that the little man in the leather jerkin and red cap suddenly appeared in their midst, and they all fell back, afraid, although they did not know why

'The wind is fair and the vessel stands ready, Skipper,' the little man said. 'Are you ready to sail, you and the lad?'

'Aye, aye,' said the skipper.

'Aye, aye, Master,' said the lad.

To the skipper's amazement, once the vessel was headed out to sea in the direction indicated by the little man, it showed no sign of sinking or shipping water: on the contrary it sped across the grey sea like some fantastic bird, its tattered rags swelling in the wind as though they were the newest and finest sails, over which a man, his wife and entire family might have laboured all winter.

Towards sunset, so fair was the wind, so smooth the passage of the vessel that the skipper found time to wonder just what cargo it was that he was carrying. Taking advantage of the fact that the little man was staring into the westering sun, he opened one of the hatches and stared down into the hold for a moment, and then drew back in alarm.

'Rats and mice!' he shouted. 'Any vessel is entitled to its quota, but this one is swarming with them.'

Turning, the little man looked at him with eyes that were as old as the grey sea itself, and then he took off his red cap and handed it to the skipper.

'Wear that and look again,' he ordered.

Now the skipper had never had anything to do with those who had lived in Scotland since the time when the world was young – the fairies whom men called the People of Peace because they feared them and their magic – but realizing that he had no choice in the matter now, he placed the

red cap on his head as he was told, and stared down into
the hold.

This time it was not rats and mice he saw, but thousands
of little creatures, all clad in woollen jerkins, long grey travelling cloaks, and wearing red caps on their straggling locks.

'Now give me back my cap,' the little man said, 'and tell
no one what you have seen, or it will be the worse for you
and for them.'

'I will tell no one,' the skipper said, glad that the boy was
busy with the sails. 'But as I have seen what I have seen, tell
me who they are and where they are bound.'

'There is no place now for the People of Peace, who are
not of the race of Adam, in the land of Scotland, so I, who
am the leader of my people, am taking them to an island
far out in the Atlantic, where we can live as we choose.'

On they sailed and on, and the stars came out and the
moon looked down on them and then, without warning, a
thick fog enveloped the vessel, and the little man told the
skipper that if he followed his instructions, the vessel would
be safe in harbour within two minutes.

Although neither the skipper nor the lad could see their
hands in front of their faces, they each followed the instructions of the little man and within two minutes they were
tying the boat up in the calm water of an unknown harbour,
still mantled in fog.

'You may both go ashore now,' the little man continued.
'Walk seven times seven paces to the north-west and seven
times seven to the north, when you will find yourselves outside a green mound, with a door facing you. The door will
be on the latch. Lift the latch and enter, but on no account
let the door close after you. Inside the mound is a vast hall,
and half way down the hall you will see a table set for two
hungry men. Eat and drink as much as you can until a storm
petrel appears at the open door and calls you three times.
Then you must arise and retrace your footsteps, and you will
find me waiting for you here.'

Now the lad was frightened, because of the many things

which those who lived near him feared, one of the greatest was walking in a thick fog over unknown ground; but the skipper knew that if he could not trust the leader of the People of Peace, he could trust no one, and as he had never harmed any of them in his life, he hoped that by doing as he was bidden, he would survive the night unharmed.

'Take my hand,' he said to the lad, 'and count as I count, and you will come to no harm.'

'I am frightened,' the boy confessed.

'You would be a fool if you were not,' the skipper answered.

So the lad took the skipper's hand and together they walked seven times seven paces to the north-west, and the ground was rocky and uneven under their feet: twice the lad stumbled and would have fallen had it not been for the steadying hand of the skipper. Then they walked seven times seven paces due west, and now there was grass under their feet, and although the skipper knew of no such island in the seas either to the north or the west of Scotland, and had begun to doubt whether he should ever see his homeland again, he said nothing of this to the lad.

As they took the last step but one, the fog lifted so that they could see they were outside a green mound with a door facing them, and the door was on the latch. Opening the door as wide as it would go, the skipper took out his clasp knife and plunged it in the grass as a door-stopper, so that the door could not blow shut while they were inside; and then, followed by the lad, he stepped into the vast hall and walked half way down to where two chairs were placed on either side of a table heaped high with every imaginable kind of delicacy.

There were all kinds of fish, salted, broiled, grilled and even baked in oatmeal; there were bowls of rich paste made from the livers of seabirds, and potted meat made from pigs' heads, and game pies with pastry which melted in the mouth, as well as soda scones, oatcakes and crisp barley bread.

'Do you think it is safe to eat such food?' the lad asked, because for long he had suspected that they were in the power of the People of Peace, who were not to be trusted.

'There is but one way to find out,' the skipper answered, and, sitting down, he helped himself to a generous portion of salt herring and ate it with gusto.

Observing that the only effect of the herring on the skipper was to whet an already keen appetite, the lad sat down opposite him, and not another word was spoken as they both ate as much as they could, and more. They were just removing the last crumbs of goats' milk cheese and washing it down with ale when a storm petrel appeared in the doorway and called them three times.

'We must go now,' the skipper said, getting to his feet and noticing that the fog had once more closed on the island so that it was impossible to see what lay beyond the door. Retrieving his clasp knife, he put it in his pocket. Then he held out his hand to the boy.

'Take it again,' he commanded, 'and count the paces in reverse and you will come to no harm.'

Slightly more confident now – for there is nothing like a good meal and good ale to make a man of a boy, and a hero of a man – the lad did as he was told: first they walked across the grass, and then across the rock, and at the last step but one they found themselves beside the vessel and the little man in his red cap awaiting them.

'The hold is empty and your work for me is done,' he said. 'Can you remember the instructions I gave you to bring the boat in here when first the fog came down?'

'I should be a poor captain if I could not remember them,' the skipper answered.

'And I should be a poor crew,' the lad added.

'Then cast off and follow them in reverse. In two minutes you will be clear of the fog, and if you are the skipper that you once were, and you, lad, the crew that you will be, you will be home in twenty-four hours, and all the better off for doing a good turn to the People of Peace. As for the boat, sink it or keep it, as you wish.'

We shall be lucky if it does not sink half-way home and

with us aboard, the skipper thought, remembering the state
the vessel was in, but he kept his thoughts to himself, because
of the lad.

'For some of the sons of Adam,' the little man continued,
'a meal such as you two have had would be payment enough,
but the People of Peace can be generous when it pleases
them.

'When you are well clear of the island, Skipper, look again
in the hold. There you will find two sacks. See that the lad
has his share of both.' With that he twisted his red cap
and disappeared before their astonished eyes.

'The sooner we are away from here, the better I shall be
pleased,' the skipper said, and following in reverse the
instruction he had been given, he took the vessel out of the
fog and breathed a sigh of relief to find himself once more
on the high seas, pausing only for a moment to marvel how
the wind had changed its quarter so that now it was blowing
them back to the shores of Scotland.

Once they were well on their course he could no longer
control his curiosity, and full of expectation of he knew not
what, climbed down into the hold with the lad after him,
and opened the first sack.

'Wood shavings,' he exclaimed, striving to conceal his
disappointment, if only for the sake of the lad.

Turning to the second sack, he opened that.

'Coal!' the lad cried, making no attempt to hide his bitter
disappointment.

'It could be worse,' the skipper said philosophically. 'At any
rate, we have both had a meal that we shall not forget in
a hurry.'

'True,' the lad agreed, 'although memory is of little use
when the belly is empty.'

On they sailed and on, each occupied with his own
thoughts, until the skipper – having had more than one
helping of salt herring in the hall in the green mound –
began to feel uncommonly thirsty.

'Lad!' he called out. 'Get a handful of wood shavings from

the first sack in the hold and brew a pot of tea, for I feel most uncommonly thirsty.'

Down into the hold the lad climbed and opened the first sack again.

'Skipper!' he cried excitedly. 'Skipper, come here at once. There are no wood shavings in the sack now.' Turning to the second sack, he opened it with trembling hands. 'And no coal either.'

When the skipper joined the lad, he saw that the first sack was filled with silver coins which winked and gleamed in the sunlight, while the second was filled with golden coins which sparkled and shone invitingly.

'The People of Peace can indeed be generous when it pleases them,' the skipper cried, letting first the silver and then the gold coins trickle through his fingers.

'The boat!' the lad cried excitedly, gazing around him and then up at the bellying sails.

'Generous, and more than generous,' the skipper exclaimed, because the boat looked as though it had been built only that season and launched the previous week: new and seasoned were its timbers, caulked its seams, and the stoutest of hand-woven sails carried them swiftly home.

Remembering what the little man had said, the skipper divided the coins equally with the lad and then, because they were both tired of living alone, they decided to build with their own hands a fine, new cottage which they would share. The skipper took the lad out to sea with him in the boat – which they also shared – and taught him all he knew on the handling of boats and the catching of fish.

Presently, the lad married a pretty fisher lass, and the skipper and the lad and the lass and all their children, lived happily ever after, thanks to the gratitude of the little man in the red cap and the People of Peace.

10

TOM THUMB

Once upon a time, in the far-off days when the great Merlin, by his magic and his wisdom, helped King Arthur to rule the land, there dwelt in a little village in Somerset a humble peasant and his wife.

They possessed one red cow, one fat pink pig, one cockerel with a scarlet comb, and five white hens. Because the peasant was hard-working and his wife clever and thrifty, they always had enough to eat and warm clothes to wear, and they would have been as happy as anyone in the land except for one thing – they had no children.

Now one morning, just as the goodwife was returning from feeding her fat, pink pig, she saw a stranger making his way down the muddy road which ran through the village, a stranger with a long, grey beard and a back bent with age.

'You look tired,' the goodwife said, noticing how heavily the old man leaned on his staff, how slowly he shuffled along. 'My cottage is a very humble one, but you are welcome to come in and sit by the fire and rest awhile.'

'Thank you, goodwife,' the stranger answered, and he followed her into her kitchen and sat down beside the fire.

'You look hungry,' the goodwife said. 'The meals we eat are very simple ones, but you are welcome to some of the soup I have made for our supper tonight.'

'Thank you, goodwife,' the stranger answered, and he took the wooden bowl on to his knee and ate the soup eagerly, as though he had not had a meal for many a long day.

A second time the goodwife filled the wooden bowl, and a third, and though the stranger had now eaten the entire meal which she had prepared for her husband and herself, she regretted nothing, feeling only pity that one so old should go so hungry.

'Thank you, goodwife,' the stranger said, when he had emptied the wooden bowl for the third time. 'For seven days and seven nights I have read in my books of magic, never resting and never eating, because King Arthur asked my help against the enemies who are planning to attack him.

'In the goodness of your heart you offered food and shelter to a poor old stranger, not knowing that he was Merlin, the Magician. I must be on my way to Camelot, where the king awaits me, but before I go – ask of me your heart's desire and you shall have it.'

'What I offered you, I would have offered any traveller,' the goodwife replied. 'But if it is really true that you can give me my heart's desire, then give me a son, O Merlin, and even if he is no bigger than my husband's thumb, there will not be a happier woman in the whole of the land.'

'A son you shall have,' Merlin agreed, and without another word he left the kitchen and set off again along the muddy road which led to distant Camelot.

'I wonder if he meant it,' the goodwife thought. 'I wonder if he really was Merlin, the Magician. Ah, well, I suppose I'd better make some more soup now.'

But the soup pot, which she herself had scraped empty, was now full to the brim.

'Oh, dear!' the goodwife cried. 'I must have dreamed it all.'

Just at that moment there came from the hearth the most entrancing cooing and chuckling and gurgling, and when the goodwife looked down, there, cradled in one of her old shoes, was a baby, no bigger than her husband's thumb.

'What a beautiful boy,' she cried, picking up the tiny baby and kissing him lovingly. And beautiful he was, with his sturdy arms and legs, and dimpled hands, and brown eyes, and brown hair the colour of an oak leaf.

Forgetting about her work, the goodwife sat by the fire

all day crooning to her baby while he cooed and chuckled and gurgled, and slept and wakened to laugh and chuckle again.

'What a fine boy,' the husband said, when he came home that night. 'But he's not very big, is he? Just the size of my thumb.'

'He'll grow in time,' the goodwife answered. 'All day, while I've been nursing him, I've been wondering what to call him, and I've come to the conclusion that the best name is – Tom.'

'Then Tom it is,' said her husband, well pleased because that happened to be his name.

'As soon as you've had your supper,' the goodwife continued, 'you must get to work and make our son a little wooden cradle while I stitch the bedclothes for it, and tomorrow I shall make him a suit of clothes.'

Nobody could have been happier than the peasant and his wife at Merlin's gift. While they wore clothes of rough homespun, they dressed Tom in the finest and softest silk, bought from a travelling pedlar, and while they ate bread and cheese, Tom was fed on eggs and butter and cream. Daily he grew more active and energetic and enterprising, and yet, in spite of all his parents' care and feeding, he never grew even a fraction of an inch, remaining always exactly the size of his father's thumb, so that when he was of an age to play with the other boys in the village, they found their own name for him which was – Tom Thumb.

Because she was frightened the village children might accidentally hurt her little son, Tom's mother tried to keep him safe with her in the cottage, but as he grew older he soon grew bored with his own company and was quick to seize every opportunity to slip out of the door and join the other boys at play.

'Where's the lad tonight?' Tom's father asked one evening as he came in from work.

'Playing with his bat and ball in the old salt-box,' Tom's mother answered.

'He's not there now,' Tom's father said.

'Where's he gone to this time?' the goodwife exclaimed.

'He's so lively and full of curiosity, there's no keeping him in the cottage. The minute my back's turned, he's off.'

Just at that moment there were loud cries of anger from the village boys who were playing at cherry-stones in the road outside the cottage, and the next minute Tom's mother heard a familiar voice cry:

'Help! Oh, help!'

'Tommy!' she cried, running outside to see Tom's head sticking out of a leather bag while one of the boys pulled the strings tighter and tighter so that Tom nearly choked.

'Leave my Tom alone,' she scolded, snatching the bag from the boy and loosening the strings so that Tom could breathe again. 'What were you doing to my son, you naughty boy?' she demanded furiously.

'I was teaching him a lesson,' the village boy answered. 'He was playing cherry-stones with us and after he lost all his own stones I caught him creeping into my bag to steal mine, so I just pulled the strings tight to teach him not to steal.'

'I wasn't stealing,' Tom wailed, as his mother carried him home, sat him on his own little three-legged stool and gave him a thimbleful of cowslip wine to revive him. 'I just wanted to find out how many cherry stones there were inside the bag.'

'Oh, Tom, you're always wanting to find out something or other,' his mother said. 'If you're not careful, you'll find yourself in real trouble one of these days.'

'I'll be careful,' Tom promised, and all the next day he played quietly underneath the table with his top and whip.

The day after that, Tom's mother decided to make a batter pudding and so she sat Tom down on the corner of the table where she could keep her eye on him and where he could watch her mixing together in a large bowl the flour and salt and eggs and milk.

'That looks just right,' she said at length. 'Now I'll go and get the pudding bag.'

'I wonder what "just right" looks like,' Tom said to himself, and as soon as his mother's back was turned, he climbed up the side of the bowl and pcered over the top.

'It looks good,' he thought. 'I wonder what it tastes like before it's cooked.'

One hand outstretched, he leaned over the rim until suddenly – plop! – he fell headfirst into the bowl and disappeared completely beneath the thick, yellow batter.

Back Tom's mother came with the pudding bag and, never noticing that Tom was no longer sitting at the corner of the table, she poured the batter into the bag, tied it at the top with a piece of string, carried it over to the fire, and dropped it into a large pan of water which she had just put on to heat.

Inside the bag, his mouth so full of batter that he couldn't utter a sound, Tom wriggled and squirmed and kicked.

He thought of the fire which burned so brightly beneath the pot. Soon it would begin to warm the water.

And the water would warm the batter.

And the batter would warm him.

And that, Tom thought, would never do and he began to wriggle and squirm and kick harder and harder and harder, so that the bag jumped about in the pot, higher and higher and higher.

'Mercy on us!' Tom's mother cried, when she saw what was happening. 'The batter's bewitched. The sooner I get rid of it, the better.' Seizing the tongs, she lifted the bag of batter out of the pot and threw it out of the window and into the street.

As it happened, a poor tinker was passing at that moment and his eyes lit up as he saw the pudding land on the ground in front of him.

'What wonderful times we live in,' he said to himself. 'Who would believe that batter puddings drop down from the sky to feed the poor and needy?' And scooping up the pudding he popped it in his pocket and hurried away with it to the nearby woods.

Sitting down on a fallen tree, he untied the string, licking his lips at the thought of the treat in store for him – and stared at the batter as though he couldn't believe his own eyes. It seemed to have a life of its own. It moved and shook and quivered; it heaved and swayed and jumped; it lurched and surged and tilted; it trembled and quaked and squirmed and joggled.

And then – in the queerest, choking kind of voice – it spoke.

It was all too much for the tinker; with a cry of terror he dropped the bag and the pudding on the ground and took to his heels and never stopped running until he reached the sea and could run no farther.

'Ugh, ugh,' Tom groaned, crawling out of the warm batter.

'Ugh, ugh,' he gurgled, trying to clear his mouth and throat.

'Ugh, ugh,' he moaned, trying to wipe the sticky batter from his hands and face and clothes with a piece of dock leaf: but the more he wiped, the harder and stickier grew the batter, so that finally he gave up in despair and set off to walk back home.

By this time his mother had discovered that her son was missing again and was looking everywhere, crying:

'Tommy, where are you? Tommy!'

'Here I am, Mother,' Tom answered, limping up to the door.

Eagerly his mother looked around, but all she could see was a blob of yellow batter, no bigger than her husband's thumb.

'Where are you?' she cried. 'I can hear you but I can't see you.'

'I'm here,' the blob of batter answered, and suddenly Tom's mother realized what had happened.

'My poor child,' she cried, picking Tom up; carrying him indoors she washed him in a cup of warm water, dried him with her handkerchief and popped him into his little bed although he kept on saying that he was quite all right.

'That's what comes of stealing the pudding,' she scolded.

'I wasn't stealing,' Tom answered. 'I just wanted to find out what it tasted like before it was cooked.'

'You're always wanting to find out something or other, Tom Thumb,' his mother said. 'If you're not careful you'll find yourself in real trouble one of these days.'

'I'll be careful,' Tom promised, and for the rest of the week he played in the cottage with the hobby horse his father had carved and painted for him.

So pleased was Tom's mother with her son's good behaviour that she decided, one evening, to take him with her when she went down to the meadow to milk the red cow. Lifting him up, she placed him in one of the two empty milking buckets, fastened the buckets to the chains at each end of the wooden yoke and fitted the yoke on to her shoulders, and then, carrying her milking stool, she set off for the meadow.

When she reached the middle of the field where the red cow was tethered, the wind was blowing so strongly that she was afraid to put Tom down on the ground in case he was blown away.

'If I'd time, I'd take you back home,' she said, 'but I haven't time, so we must make the best of it,' and pulling out one of her long, black hairs, she tied one end round Tom's waist and the other round a sturdy thistle which was growing nearby. 'Now sit there quietly and don't annoy the red cow while I'm milking her,' she said.

For a little while Tom sat quietly where his mother had put him, keeping well away from the sharp spikes of the thistle; around him the tall grass swayed and bent and sighed in the wind while from far above came the soft swish of the milk as it filled the wooden bucket.

'Milk,' Tom said to himself. 'I wonder what it tastes like before it's cooled in the dairy.' Pulling and tugging at the hair which tied him to the thistle, Tom wriggled in and out of the thick blades of grass, searching for the milking bucket.

Far, far above him, the red cow caught a glimpse of something brown moving in the green grass.

'Looks like an oak leaf,' she said, suddenly feeling hungry, and, bending down, she put out her tongue, scooped Tom up in her big, red mouth and started munching and chewing.

'Help!' Tom cried. 'Help, oh, help!'

'Where are you, Tommy?' his mother cried in alarm.

'I'm here, Mother,' a muffled voice answered.

Anxiously his mother looked around, but all she could see was the red cow munching and chewing.

'Where are? I can hear you but I can't see you.'

'I'm inside the red cow's mouth,' Tom wailed.

'Mercy on us!' his mother cried, springing up so suddenly that she knocked over the bucket and all the milk soaked away in the grass. 'Oh, what shall I do? Whatever shall I do?'

Inside the red cow's mouth Tom began to beat his fists, and kick, and shout at the top of his voice, so that before very long she opened her mouth to give an angry moo: immediately Tom seized his chance and jumped out and his mother was only just in time to catch him in her apron. Holding him to her tightly, she ran all the way home, washed him in a cup of warm water, dried him with her handkerchief, and popped him into his little bed although he kept on saying that he was quite all right.

'That's what comes of stealing the milk,' she scolded.

'I wasn't stealing,' Tom answered. 'I just wanted to find out what it was like before it was cooled.'

'You're always wanting to find out something or other, Tom Thumb,' his mother said. 'If you're not careful you'll find yourself in real trouble one of these days.'

'I'll be careful,' Tom promised, and for the rest of the month he sat on the doorstep where his mother could see him and played merry tunes on the pipes his father had made for him.

So pleased was Tom's father with his son's behaviour that he decided, one fine morning, to take Tom with him when he went to move the farmer's cattle from one field to another. He made Tom a whip from a piece of barley straw and a length of cotton and off he went, with Tom running and skipping behind him and not looking where he was going, so that he tumbled head over heels into the first furrow, and lay there on his back, stunned and breathless.

On walked Tom's father, not realizing that Tom was no longer following, and a raven flying far above in the blue sky gave a caw of triumph as she spied the little creature lying in the furrowed field; down she swooped, and when she rose again she had Tom in her curved beak.

'Help!' Tom shrieked in alarm as he found himself carried up into the skies. 'Help, oh, help!'

He kicked and he wriggled and he squirmed; he shouted at the top of his voice and he beat on the raven's beak with his clenched fists until at last the bird opened her mouth to give a squawk of anger. Immediately Tom seized his chance and jumped out, but this time there was no mother to catch him in her apron, and down he dropped from the blue sky, down and down and down, with the song of the wind in his ears, down and down and down – until – at last –

Splash!

And Tom found himself in the sea, sinking down again and down, until at last he landed on the sand at the very bottom.

'Where have you come from?' a seahorse neighed, gaping at Tom as he galloped past.

'Who are you?' a sea anemone squeaked, waving her long grey-green tentacles angrily.

'You look a tasty morsel,' a great sturgeon thundered, and he opened wide his mouth and swallowed Tom whole.

'Help!' Tom cried. 'Help, oh, help!' He kicked and wriggled and squirmed, and beat with his clenched fists, but the sturgeon just grunted and swallowed, and down poor Tom Thumb slid, right into the fish's stomach.

On through the green sea swam the great sturgeon, and presently he spied another tasty morsel, which he swallowed so hastily that only when it was too late did he realize he had swallowed a hook as well, and that he had been caught by a fisherman in a boat above.

When the fisherman saw what it was that he had landed, he was delighted, because he knew that the sturgeon was fish royal, and had to be offered to the King, who would reward him generously.

Back to the coast he rowed and, wrapping the great fish in seaweed, he placed it in a basket and set off for the King's Court at Camelot, where he was well paid for his catch.

'A fine fish,' said the cook, sharpening her knife. Skilfully she cut open the sturgeon, and then she gave a cry of fright; the knife clattered on to the stone floor and all the scullions and maidservants and menservants came running to see what was the matter.

'Look,' the cook whispered, pointing with a trembling finger. 'It is not fish royal; it is fish bewitched.'

Eyes wide with astonishment, everyone watched the fish as it moved and shook and quivered, heaved and swayed and jumped, lurched and surged and tilted, trembled and quaked and squirmed and joggled ... until ... at last ... out crept ... poor little Tom Thumb.

'Mercy on us!' the cook cried. 'It's a boy.' Picking Tom up, she washed him in a cup of warm water, dried him on the corner of her apron, and put him down in the middle of the table where everyone could admire him.

'King Arthur must see this fine fellow,' she said, setting to and baking a mutton pie with layers of mutton and layers of apple and a good grating of nutmeg to flavour it. When it was cold, she made a hole in the top of the crust, popped Tom through it, and carried the pie into the hall where King Arthur sat at the Round Table, feasting with his Queen and his Knights and their Ladies.

'Mutton pie!' said King Arthur, smacking his lips, and he cut himself a large slice and put it on his plate.

'Mercy on us!' exclaimed the Queen, staring at the rest of the pie. 'I'm sure I saw something move there.'

'It's only me,' Tom cried, jumping out of the pie and down on to the table, where he bowed to the King and to the Queen, and finally to the Knights and all their Ladies.

'What is your name?' King Arthur asked, 'and how did you get into my mutton pie?'

'My name is Tom Thumb,' Tom answered, 'and I got into your pie because I tripped over a furrow, and a raven picked me up and was taking me home for her dinner until I made such a fuss that she dropped me in the sea; there a sturgeon swallowed me, but a fisherman caught the sturgeon and brought it to your cook, and when she cut it open, I jumped out.'

'What an adventurous life,' the Knights exclaimed.

'What a handsome fellow,' the Ladies whispered.

'Tell me more about yourself,' King Arthur commanded, and so lively and amusing did Tom make his adventures, that the King offered him a position in his court, promising at the same time to send a bar of gold each year to Tom's parents, so that they should not want for anything.

Once Tom was a courtier, he needed new clothes to fit his rank so the Queen and her Ladies set to work; they spun him hose from the shimmering moonbeams, a cape from the soft cobwebs and a shirt from the wings of the blue dragon-fly.

So popular did he become that before long King Arthur decided to make him a knight, and for the ceremony the Queen fashioned him a helmet from her thimble and a sword from her darning needle, and she mounted him on a splendid steed – a tame white mouse, called Sukey.

As Tom grew more bold and adventurous and travelled far and wide throughout the kingdom, the journeys were too much for Sukey, who was used to the luxury of palace life, and so the Queen ordered a special coach of the purest gold to be made for Tom, and the coach was drawn by six small white mice who were chosen for their strength and speed.

Popularity never spoiled Tom and never did he forget his father and mother. Once every year, on his birthday, Sir Thomas Thumb jumped into his golden coach, flourished his whip above the six white mice, and amidst the cheers of the courtiers and the people of Camelot he drove off to the little village where his parents awaited him so eagerly.

'You know,' his mother would say as she kissed him fondly,

'I always said that if I had a son no bigger than your father's thumb, I should be perfectly happy. And I am.'

'And so am I,' said Tom's father.

'And so am I,' said Tom.

Far away in his castle in the Welsh Mountains, Merlin lifted his head from his books of magic and gazed into the crystal ball beside him, and there he saw Tom and his father and mother smiling happily at one another.

'Tomorrow I must write down the entire history of Tom Thumb,' he said to himself, 'so that a thousand years from now, children can still read about him; it's a story that they'll all like because it's full of adventures and in the end, everyone lives happily ever after.'

11

THE LAD IN SEARCH OF A FORTUNE

Once upon a time there was a farmer's lad who was always hard-working and happy. Year in, year out, he whistled and sang cheerfully. But one spring as the birdsong grew louder, he grew quieter, and at last the only sound that escaped his lips was an occasional long, long sigh.

Finally, on a bright May morning when the skylark sang high in the sky and the ring dove cooed amongst the pear tree blossom, the lad spoke his mind to the farmer.

'Gaffer,' he said, 'you've always been a good master to me, but the time has come when I must leave you and seek my fortune. I mean to rescue a beautiful maiden in distress. Her father will then reward me with half his wealth and lands and her hand in marriage, and we shall live happily ever after.'

'The May sunshine has always addled the wits of young men,' the farmer replied. 'But you've always been a good lad, and so if things don't turn out as you expect, come back here and I'll double your wages, give you a thatched cottage, a fine pig, a goat and six speckled hens.'

The lad thanked the farmer, put some bread in his pocket and set off. Over hill and dale he walked until he came to a field where children laughed and chattered as they gathered flowers, all too busy to notice one little girl who sat by herself and wept bitterly.

'What is the matter, child?' the lad asked.

'Today we gather May flowers to make knots and posies for our mothers,' the child answered, 'but I fell down and crushed my flowers and now I am too tired to pick any more.'

'We'll soon put that right,' the lad said cheerfully, and he gathered pink ragged robin and bluebells, silver milkmaids and heartsease, and wrapped them in the green leaves of moonwort.

Without a word of thanks the child took the May knot, but she broke off a stalk of the green fern.

'Keep this moonwort,' she said, 'and you will not rue our meeting.' And off she ran.

As the lad had not found his fortune when the sun set, he ate some of his bread, drank from a nearby stream, and fell fast asleep under a hawthorn, its clusters of cream flowers scenting the night air.

On the second day he set off again over hill and dale until he came to a well garlanded with herb paris and pink clover, primroses and ox-eye daisies. Beside it sat an old woman, lamenting loudly.

'What is the matter, old woman?' the lad asked.

'Everyone was so busy decorating our well today that no one filled my pitcher,' the old woman answered.

'We'll soon put that right,' the lad said confidently, and he filled the pitcher to the brim. Without a word of thanks the old woman took it, but she poured some of the water into a leather bottle.

'Take it,' she said, 'and you will not rue our meeting,' and off she hobbled.

As the lad had still not found his fortune when the sun set, he ate some more of his bread, drank from a chattering brook, and fell fast asleep under an oak, green with new, young leaves.

On the third day he set off again over hill and dale until he came to a village where a maypole had been set up on the green. An old man tuned his fiddle and the lads chose their partners for the dance, paying no attention to an ill-favoured lass who stood apart and sighed.

'What is the matter, lass?' the lad asked.

'No one will ask me to dance because I haven't a pretty face,' the lass answered.

'We'll soon put that right,' the lad said gently. Leading

the lass to the centre of the green he picked up the last two ribbons, and joining the others, they danced round and round and in and out, winding and then unwinding the coloured ribbons round the tall maypole.

When at last the dance was over, the lass disappeared without a word of thanks, and the lad went on his way.

So intent was he on seeking his fortune that he did not notice the lass following him, nor, when the sun set and he fell asleep under a wild crab, did he know that she curled up beside him.

The next morning he was awakened by rough hands shaking him and the angry voice of the lord of the manor shouting that it was time rogues and vagabonds were taught a lesson.

'Throw them both into prison,' the lord commanded. 'Tomorrow beat them both soundly and then drive them off my land.'

Before the lad could protest that he was neither rogue nor vagabond, he found himself locked in a dark cell with the ill-favoured lass beside him.

'Oh, dear,' he sighed. 'I'm footsore and hungry and tomorrow I shall be beaten soundly. If only I could get out of here I'd go straight back to the Gaffer and never have such foolish dreams again.'

'What is that fern that peeps out of your pocket?' the lass asked.

'Moonwort,' he answered.

'Every good country lass knows that moonwort opens locks,' the lass said, and she waved the fern in front of the prison door. Immediately it swung open. Hand in hand they ran out of the prison and kept on running until they had left the lands of the bad-tempered lord far behind.

'I'm tired and I'm hot and I'm thirsty,' the lad said, as they sat down wearily in a green meadow.

'What have you got in your leather bottle?' the lass asked. 'Water,' the lad replied, taking out the stopper and pouring some into the lass's cupped hands.

'Every good country lass knows this came from a wishing-well,' the lass said, and while the lad drank, she bathed her face in the clear water.

What they wished I don't know, but when the lad looked up he saw before him the most beautiful maiden in the whole world, and he realized he wouldn't know a moment's happiness until he had made her his wife.

He made a chain of daisies, and set them as a crown on her corn-gold hair. He made a ring from a long-stemmed butter-cup, and put it on the third finger of her left hand and then he led her proudly back to the farm.

Perhaps she had no rich father to give him half his wealth and lands and to keep him in idle luxury: certainly it was her quick wits that had saved him, but as she could card and spin, weave and sew, milk and churn, he knew he needed no greater fortune. And as they both loved each other dearly, they lived happily ever after in the thatched cottage with the pig and the goat and the six speckled hens.

12

THE WIDOW AND THE
HEDLEY KOW

Once upon a time a poor widow lived in a tumble-down cottage not far from the village of Hedley, in the North of England.

As she had no money to pay anyone to do repairs, the wind whistled through the cracks in the walls and windows, and the rain dripped through the holes in the roof.

All the furniture she possessed was a three-legged stool which her father had made for her when she was a child. For a bed, she used such straw as the farmers could spare when she helped them in the fields, and she rose early each morning to gather fallen branches and pine cones for her fire.

Each day she found some kind of work to do in the village in exchange for her midday meal, and each evening she would return with something for her supper, even if it were only a slice of dry bread or a piece of stale cheese.

Although she was poor, she never grumbled or complained. Whatever happened, she always made the best of things, and the people of Hedley said it did them good just to see her smiling face.

Now in those days there were all manner of witches and fairies and goblins about. Some were good. And some were not. As most of them wandered about when it was dark, the widow always made a point of returning home before night fell. However, one Saturday night her work took longer than she expected, and the stars were beginning to appear, one by one, as she arranged her shawl and tied on her bonnet.

'Hurry straight home, and don't stop, no matter what happens,' the village women said. 'The Hedley Kow is up to his tricks again. He changes himself into all kinds of shapes to confuse people and frighten them, and then he laughs at them and runs away.'

'I'm not frightened of the Hedley Kow, or of any other goblin,' the widow answered, and she set off down the lonely lane to her cottage.

She hadn't gone very far when she saw something lying in the middle of the lane. Drawing closer, she looked at it in amazement, and then she began to laugh.

'Well, I never, hinny!' she cried. 'A whole leg of roast pork with the most delicious crackling.' And she looked up the lane and down the lane, but there was no one there who could have dropped it. 'Why, that's exactly what I've been wanting to eat for many a long year.'

Picking up the leg of roast pork, she wrapped it in her apron, and, carrying it very carefully, she walked on.

She hadn't gone very far before she realized that with each step she took the pork was growing heavier and heavier, until in the end she could no longer carry it.

Carefully she placed it on the ground, unwrapped her apron, and then began to laugh.

'Well, I never, hinny!' she cried. 'It isn't a leg of pork at all. It's a fine table made of the very best oak. Why, that's exactly what I've been wanting for many a long year.'

She turned the table upside down, balanced it on her head, and walked on.

She hadn't gone very far before she realized that with each step she took the table was growing heavier and heavier, until in the end she could no longer carry it.

Lowering it to the ground, she stared at it in amazement, and then she began to laugh.

'Well, I never, hinny!' she cried. 'It isn't a table at all. It's a bundle of straw. And that's exactly what I've been wanting to sleep on for many a long week.'

Picking up the straw, she tucked it under one arm and walked on. And on. And on.

It was just when she reached her cottage that she realized the straw was too heavy for her to carry any longer.

She lowered it to the ground, and then stared at it in amazement.

'Well, I never, hinny!' she cried. 'It isn't a bundle of straw at all. It's a great big boulder. And that is exactly what I've been wanting to stop my door blowing open on windy nights.'

The boulder quivered. And wriggled. And shook. And shivered.

The next moment it disappeared, and in its place was a strange, long-legged creature dressed in green, who scowled at the widow, put out his tongue, waggled his big, pointed ears and laughed mockingly.

'Well, I never, hinny!' the widow cried. 'At last I've seen the Hedley Kow. That's exactly what I've been wanting to see all my life. Oh, won't people be interested when I tell them.'

The Hedley Kow stopped laughing and pulling faces.

'Aren't you frightened of me?' he asked, in a very disappointed voice.

'Of course not,' the widow answered.

'Everyone else is,' the goblin pointed out.

The widow smiled – a nice, kind smile.

'Why don't you come in and share my supper?' she asked. 'I've got a bowl of milk curds and a slice of rye bread.'

'Well, I never, hinny!' the Hedley Kow said. 'No one's ever asked me to share their supper before,' and he hurried after the widow into the cottage.

As she had only one stool, one plate, one bowl and one spoon, they took it in turns to sit down and to dip the spoon in the bowl of delicious milk curds, and to nibble the rye bread.

After that they talked. At least the Hedley Kow talked and the widow listened.

On the stroke of midnight, the widow yawned, and the Hedley Kow sighed.

And vanished.

But that's not the end of the tale. Oh, no!

The next evening the Hedley Kow started to work.

First of all he stopped up the cracks in the walls and windows of the widow's cottage so that the wind couldn't get in. Then he repaired the roof to keep out the rain.

I've never been so happy in all my long life, he thought, and each night, as soon as it was dark, he skipped off from cottage to mill, from bakehouse to farm – sweeping and scrubbing and cleaning and repairing.

So pleased was everyone with his work that they always left food and cream and kindling for him.

Half of what he got, he placed each morning on the widow's doorstep; and every Saturday evening he knocked on the door, and the widow opened it with cries of pleasure, and together they ate and talked and laughed.

'What a lucky woman I was to meet the Hedley Kow,' the widow often said. But everyone else thought the Hedley Kow was lucky to meet the widow – don't you?

13

THE FAIR PRINCE AND
HIS BROTHERS

Once upon a time, in the far north of the country which we now call Scotland, there lived in a grim, grey stone castle, a powerful king and his three sons. The two elder were red of hair and their eyes were as green as the moss that grows on the border of the treacherous bog, but the youngest had hair as yellow as the oats before they were cut in the late summer, and his eyes were as blue as the waters of a lochan on a rare sunny morning.

In days of peace, nothing delighted the king more than to ride forth accompanied by his men and his three sons, each with his own hound and his own hawk, to hunt venison or bring down pheasants and duck, partridges and grouse, to provide food for themselves and their hungry people.

But what delighted the king most of all was when some quarrel sprang up between his neighbours and himself: then the hounds would be kennelled, the hawks chained by one leg to their platform in their out-houses, and the king and his sons would ride forth, armed with swords and daggers, shouting defiance to the sullen skies, vowing to fight and maim and kill and return home with rich booty and many captives.

All except the younger son – he of the fair hair and blue eyes. Birds and beasts must be killed so that man might live, he said, but he could see no reason why man should kill his own kind: and in spite of his father's blows and the elder brothers' jeers, he would mount his horse, ride off at a gallop, and only stop when he could help the old men, the women and children who were left to tend the fields and beasts, or aid the fisher-lads land their catch to feed such of the hungry fighters as might return from the battle.

'He is no son of mine!' the king shouted, when he found that neither threats nor bribes could alter the mind of his youngest son. 'Never let me see his face again.' And he did his best to ignore the boy when they were out hunting, or eating at the long table in the Great Hall, or gathered round the fire listening to the minstrel as he sang of the heroic deeds of their ancestors.

However, the day came when the eldest son approached his father, his face dark and sullen.

'Father,' he said, 'I am weary of hunting, and as for fighting, I have either killed all my enemies or else they flee and take to their boats as soon as they get word of my approach. I have come to ask permission to leave the castle and go in search of adventure. All I need is a little food, my horse, Midnight, my hound, Marvel, and my hawk, Mandrake.'

Comforting himself that his second son would still be in the castle to sally forth with him and do battle, the king gave his permission, and the eldest son rode off on his coal-black horse, Midnight, with Marvel, his black wolf hound, trotting along beside, and Mandrake, his black-hooded hawk, perched on his gauntleted wrist.

For three days he alternately rode and walked, passing well beyond the boundary of his father's kingdom. His hawk, his hound, and his horse and he himself had consumed all their provisions as they crossed moorland bog, heather and bracken. Following a peaty burn, he came at last to a steep pass sliced between two bare mountains, and just as the sun began to sink and his shadow to lengthen so that it might have been that of a giant, he reached the top of the pass and saw lying in the glen below a humble cottage thatched with turf, with a tumble-down barn behind it. Urging on his horse and hound, he reached the cottage just as the cold damp mists of night closed in on him.

'Is anyone in?' he shouted, knocking loudly on the door. A second time he called, and a third, and when there was still no answer, he flung open the door, strode in and looked around.

A cauldron of venison and rabbit simmered above a low fire: against one wall a rush basket held six turves of peat, and on a rough-hewn table were two wooden bowls and a jug of water.

Whoever lives here must have been expecting me, he thought, and leaving Midnight, Marvel and Mandrake to settle down in the darkest corner – unfed, unwatered and uncared for – he threw all the peat on the fire and helped himself to the broth and the water until both cauldron and jug were empty. Grunting with satisfaction, he wrapped his thick woollen plaid round him, placed his sword within an inch of his right hand, and fell asleep in front of the fire.

At midnight he awoke suddenly and, grabbing his sword, sat up and stared at the wrinkled old woman who stood in the open door, white elfin locks blowing round her head and shoulders.

'So ye warmed yourself?' she said, looking at the glowing fire and the empty peat basket.

'Aye,' he answered, annoyed at being wakened up.

'And ye quenched your thirst?' she said, looking at the empty jug.

'Aye.'

'And ye fed yourself?' she said, peering into the empty cauldron.

'Aye.' And the eldest son was just preparing to go to sleep again when the old woman saw the shadowy forms of Midnight, Marvel and Mandrake in the far corner of the cottage.

'Does your horse kick?' she demanded.

'Aye.'

'Fling that over him,' she ordered, pulling a long white hair from her head. And the eldest son, feeling tired and wanting to go to sleep again, did as he was told.

'Does your hound bite?' she demanded.

'Aye.'

'Fling that over him,' she ordered, pulling a second white hair from her head. And he did as he was told.

'Does your hawk tear with his curved beak?' she demanded.

'Aye.'

'Fling that over him,' she ordered, pulling out a third white hair, and again he did as he was told.

'Fool! Fool! Fool!' she screamed, and as he found he was powerless to move, she grabbed a chopper from behind the door, and chopped off the eldest son's head, while his horse and his hound and his hawk stood motionless, as though they had been turned to stone.

*   *   *

Time passed, and at length came the day when the second son, his face dark and sullen, approached his father.

'Father,' he said, 'I am weary of hunting and fighting. I have come to ask permission to leave the castle and go in search of adventure. All I need is a little food, my horse, Demon, my hound, Dancer, and my hawk, Diamond.'

Hoping that it would not be long before his eldest son returned, the king gave permission, and the second son rode off on his chestnut-brown horse, Demon, with Dancer, his brown hound, trotting along beside him, and Diamond, his brown-hooded hawk, perched on his gauntleted wrist.

For three days the second son alternately rode and walked, and just as the cold damp mists of the fourth night closed in, he came to the humble cottage thatched with turf. Paying no attention to the locked barn behind the cottage, he knocked three times on the door, and when there was no answer, he strode in and looked around.

Whoever lives here must have been expecting me, he said to himself, looking from the rush basket with its six turves of peat to the two wooden bowls and the jug of water, and smelling the delicious aroma of the broth in the cauldron.

Leaving Demon, Dancer and Diamond to settle down in the darkest corner – unfed, unwatered and uncared for – he threw all the peat on the fire and helped himself to the broth and the water until both cauldron and jug were empty. Grunting with satisfaction, he wrapped his thick woollen plaid round him, placed his sword within an inch of his right hand, and fell asleep in front of the fire.

At midnight he awoke suddenly, and grabbing his sword, sat up and stared at the wrinkled old woman who stood in the open door, white elfin locks blowing round her head and shoulders.

'So ye warmed yourself?' she said, looking at the glowing fire and the empty peat basket.

'Aye,' he answered, annoyed at being wakened up.

'And ye quenched your thirst?' she said, looking at the empty jug.

'Aye.'

'And ye fed yourself?' she said, peering into the empty cauldron.

'Aye.' And the second son was just preparing to go to sleep again when the old woman saw the shadowy forms of Demon, Dancer and Diamond in the far corner of the cottage.

'Does your horse kick?' she demanded.

'Aye.'

'Fling that over him,' she ordered, pulling a long white hair from her head, and so tired and sleepy was he, that he did as he was told.

'Does your hound bite?' she demanded.

'Aye.'

'Fling that over him,' she ordered, pulling a second white hair from her head. And he did as he was told.

'Does your hawk tear with his curved beak?' she demanded.

'Aye.'

'Fling that over him,' she ordered, pulling out a third white hair, and again he did as he was told.

'Fool! Fool! Fool!' she screamed, and as he found he was powerless to move, she grabbed a chopper from behind the door and chopped off his head, while his horse and his hound and his hawk stood motionless, as though they had been turned to stone.

*   *   *

Time passed. The king grew old and lost all interest in wars and hunting now that his two favourite sons were no longer with him. When at last he took to his bed and refused all potions and all sustaining foods, the physicians shook their heads gravely.

'He will die as surely as winter follows on the heels of autumn,' they said, 'unless ...'

'Unless what?' the youngest son asked.

'Unless his two elder sons return within a week and a day,' they pronounced gravely.

So it was that, with a humble and loving look, the youngest son approached his father's bed.

'Father,' he said, 'for reasons of my own, grant me permission to leave the castle for but a short space. All I need is a little food for myself and for my white mare, Jennet, my white dog, Jewel, and my white falcon, Jessamine.'

'You have always gone your own way as a boy, why ask for permission to leave now?' the king asked bitterly, and, closing his eyes, he turned his face to the wall.

For three days the youngest son alternately rode and walked, and just as the cold, damp mists of the fourth night closed in, he came to the humble cottage thatched with turf, and wondered why the barn behind it was so securely locked.

Three times he knocked on the cottage door, and when there was no answer, he opened the door gently and walked in.

Whoever lives here must expect benighted travellers, he thought, looking from the rush basket with its six turves of peat to the two wooden bowls and the jug of water, and savouring the delicious smell of the broth in the cauldron. First, however, he fed and watered Jennet, his mare, then he gave Jewel, his dog, all the provisions he himself had not eaten, and finally he unhooded Jessamine and gave her the pigeon she had brought down earlier that day. Only when his three companions were satisfied, and he had whispered his thanks to them for their companionship on the journey, did the youngest son think about himself.

Dipping one of the wooden bowls in the cauldron and blowing on it to cool it, he drank it slowly, savouring each mouthful. Enough is as good as a feast, he thought, and he drank the water in the jug and then went to the stream outside, refilled the jug, and brought in some fallen branches to mend the fire. With a sigh of content he wrapped his plaid around him and fell fast asleep in front of the fire.

At midnight he awoke suddenly and sat up, to see an old woman standing in the doorway, her white, elfin locks blowing around her head and shoulders.

'So ye warmed yourself?' she said, looking at the fire and scowling as she saw the basket still full of peat.

'Aye, and thank ye for your hospitality,' the youngest son answered.

'And ye quenched your thirst?' she said, looking at the jug which the youngest son had filled so full of water that a drop had spilled on to the table.

'Aye, and thank ye for your hospitality,' the youngest son said.

'And ye fed yourself?' she said, peering into the cauldron.

'Aye. Maybe ye will let Jessamine bring ye a brace of fine birds tomorrow to replenish your broth?'

Immediately the old woman swung round and saw the shadowy figures of Jennet, Jewel and Jessamine.

'Does your mare kick?' she demanded.

'Aye.'

'Fling that over her,' she ordered, pulling a long white hair from her head, but Jennet looked first at her master, and then at the fire, and the youngest son threw the hair among the flames, where it crackled and burned.

'What is that crackling?' the old woman asked suspiciously.

'It's only the green wood I used to mend the fire,' the youngest son answered, and the old woman was satisfied.

'Does your hound bite?' she demanded.

'Aye.'

'Fling that over him,' she ordered, pulling a second white hair from her head, but Jewel looked first at his master and

then at the fire, and the youngest son threw the hair among the flames, where it crackled and burned.

'What is that crackling?' the old woman croaked.

'Only the green wood I used to mend the fire.' And again the old woman was satisfied.

'Does you hawk tear with her curved beak?'

'Aye.'

'Fling that over her,' she ordered, pulling out a third white hair, but Jessamine looked first at her master and then at the fire, and the youngest son threw the third hair among the flames, where it crackled and burned.

'Fool! Fool! Fool!' the old witch screamed – for witch indeed she was – and she reached for the chopper, but the youngest son was ready for her.

'Kick her, Jennet, my mare!' he cried. 'Bite her, Jewel, my dog. Tear out her hair, Jessamine, my hawk.'

When the witch realized she had lost her power, that her wicked spells no longer worked, she gave a loud shriek of despair, and before the eyes of the astonished son she shrank ... and dwindled ... and crumbled ... until there was only a little heap of dust where she had been standing. At that moment there was an end to all her witchcraft, and from the barn appeared the two brothers, strong and healthy, their heads on their necks – where, of course, they ought to be – and accompanied by their horses, their hounds and their hawks.

During the long months when they had been turned to stone, they realized how selfish they had been, and now they embraced their brother with gratitude and affection and promised faithfully that they would think of their brother and their people first, and themselves last.

When the sentinel on the castle walls saw the three brothers riding home with their hounds and their hawks, he hurried to the king, who immediately ordered three basins of whipped eggs and goats' milk to fortify him, then he left his bed and gave orders for a banquet to be prepared in the Great Hall, donned his richest garments, and went to the gate to welcome them, tears of joy streaming down his cheeks.

When he heard the full story of the adventure, he wept again.

'Three sons I have,' he said. 'Each different and each as dear to me as life itself. I am an old man now, no longer fit for hunting and fighting: I shall divide my land into three parts, so that each will rule according to his nature and desire.' And so it was that the king and the princes – and the beautiful princesses whom later they married – all lived happily ever after.